Unlaced
AT
CHRISTMAS

Unlaced
AT
CHRISTMAS

Christine
MERRILL

Linda
SKYE

Elizabeth
ROLLS

Published in Great Britain 2015
by Mills & Boon, an imprint of Harlequin (UK) Limited,
Eton House, 18-24 Paradise Road, Richmond, Surrey, TW9 1SR

UNLACED AT CHRISTMAS © 2015 Harlequin Books S.A.

The Christmas Duchess © 2014 Christine Merrill
Russian Winter Nights © 2013 Linda Skye
A Shocking Proposition © 2014 Elizabeth Rolls

ISBN: 978-0-263-91566-2

011-1015

Harlequin (UK) Limited's policy is to use papers that are natural, renewable and recyclable products and made from wood grown in sustainable forests.The logging and manufacturing processes conform to the legalenvironmental regulations of the country of origin.

Printed and bound in Spain
by CPI, Barcelona

ROM
Pbk

THE CHRISTMAS DUCHESS

Christine Merrill

Christine Merrill lives on a farm in Wisconsin, USA, with her husband, two sons, and too many pets—all of whom would like her to get off the computer so they can check their e-mail. She has worked by turns in theatre costuming and as a librarian. Writing historical romance combines her love of good stories and fancy dress with her ability to stare out of the window and make stuff up.

Chapter One

Generva Marsh gave the kitchen a final sweep and sighed in resignation. It was not her job to be keeping her own house. Mrs Jordan, the housekeeper, would disapprove of her meddling. But Mrs Jordan was above stairs, transfixed by the wailing and lamentations coming from Gwendolyn's bedroom. Generva had been more than happy to abdicate that role. The girl had cried nonstop since Sunday, and the sound preyed upon her nerves.

Perhaps it was unmotherly to admit such a lack of sympathy for one's only daughter. Perhaps the ladylike response to the chaos surrounding them was to have a fit of vapours. She should shut herself up in a bedchamber, as Gwen was doing, and turn the whole house upside down. But it was still a damned nuisance. It might be mortifying when one's gentleman proved himself to be no gentleman at all. But when it happened before the wedding and not after, it was cause for celebration and not tears. It would have been far worse had they married.

Perhaps it was her own, dear, John who had given Generva such an annoyingly sensible attitude. When one was the widow of a ship's captain, one learned to sail on through adversity and live each day prepared for the worst. When she had lost him, she had cried for a day as if her heart would break. Then she had looked at her two children and dried her tears so she could wipe theirs.

Now she must do so again, for one child, at least. Little Benjamin did not need her help. When he had heard the news he had declared it good riddance, stolen one of the mince pies she'd set aside for the wedding breakfast and disappeared into the yard. Generva frowned. The boy was a terror, but at least he was out of the way. The girl could have one more day, at most, to sulk over the unexpected turn things had taken.

Then she would be ordered to pull herself together, wash her face and prepare to meet the village on Christmas morning. The congregation had been promised a wedding at the end of the service. Instead, the Marshes would be proving a veritable morality play on the dangers of pride and youthful folly. They would be forced to hold their heads high and accept the condolences of the town gossips who smiled behind their hands even as they announced that it was, 'a terrible, terrible shame, that such a lovely girl was tainted by scandal'. The old women would cluck like chickens and the young men would look away from them in embarrassment, as though Gwen was something more than an innocent victim of another's perfidy.

Generva's hands tightened on the handle of the broom. If John were still alive, he'd have called the fellow out. Men were far more sensible in that way than women. They saw such problems and found a solution. But as the widowed mother of the wronged girl, there was little society would permit her to do, other than wring her hands and bear her share of the disgrace.

'*In dulci jubilo...*' From the road outside, she heard the sound of a deep voice raised in song.

For a moment, she paused to lean on the broom and listen. John would have declared the fellow to have 'a fine set of lungs' and thrown open the door to him and any friends who accompanied him. Then he'd have poured drinks from the hearth and matched them verse for verse with his own fine tenor voice. He'd told her that, for a sailor on land, a good, old-fashioned Christmas wassail was as near to grog and shanties as one could hope.

She smiled for a moment, then glanced at the empty pot beside the kitchen fire. It was a lost tradition in this household. If a widow did not want to incite gossip, she did not open the house to misrule and invite strangers to drink punch in the kitchen. She missed it all the same.

'There was a pig went out to dig, on Christmas Day, on Christmas Day...' The singer had finished his first song and gone on to another. He sang alone, but the carol was suited to a troupe. It had been an age since she had seen mummers in the area, putting on skits and begging door to door. It harked back to an earlier time, when Christmas was little more than a chaotic revel. Right now, she could imagine nothing more pleasant than throwing off the conventions of society and running wild.

She forced the thought to the back of her mind. Someone must keep a cool head while they weathered the current disaster. It would be her, since she could not count on her daughter, her son or her servants to behave in a rational manner. She had no time or money to spare for seasonal beggars. Nor did she have the patience. The wedding feast she had been preparing for nearly a month would go to charity. Surely that was enough of a holiday offering. When the housekeeper came to get her, if that woman could tear herself away from the drama upstairs to answer the door, Generva would plead a megrim and tell her to send the caroller away.

She heard the distant sound of the knocker at the front of the house and waited for the inevitable. But then, the song began again, growing louder as the singer rounded the corner of the house. 'There was a crow went out to sow...' She saw the shadow of a large body passing the window and there was a pounding on the back door.

She turned away, so that he might not know she had seen him. Damn the man and his industrious animals. She began to sweep again with more vigour. Perhaps he would think her deaf and move on to the next house.

Behind her, she felt the rush of cold air at the opening of the kitchen door. 'Hallo! Is anyone there? I knocked at the front, but there was no answer. Is there a drink for a humble traveller who bears good news?'

She sighed. Was no one in this house tending to their posts? Was everything to be left to her? She turned back to the short hall that led to the back door and found it full of man.

Perhaps there was a better way to describe it, but she could not think of one. The gentleman standing by the door was tall and broad shouldered, and seemed to occupy all of the available space. What was not full of his body was crowded with the sheer force of his personality. The voice that had called out had not simply spoken, it had boomed. It had not been particularly loud, but deep and resonant. There was none of the awkwardness in his step of a man uncomfortable in unfamiliar surroundings. He approached as if he owned the room.

And it appeared that he could afford to do so. She had expected some beggar in a tattered mask. But the cost of this man's coat, with its perfect tailoring and shiny brass buttons, was probably near to the annual rent of her cottage. His boots were equal to a second year. Slowly, she raised her eyes to look into his.

They were the blue of moonlit snow, bright and clear, but not cold, or even cool. They sparkled like the first drop of water on thawing ice. Perhaps it was his smile that brought the beginning of spring. It was soft and warm, seeming to light his whole person, making him seem young for his years, as though the silver in his black hair would melt away like hoarfrost. His face was as well formed as his body: high cheeks, even planes, strong chin and a nose that was regally straight but without the disdainful flare of nostrils that some rich men had when entering a simple house such as hers.

She was gawping at him and embarrassing herself. At five and thirty, she should be past the point of noticing the finer points of the male physique. She had two children to tend to and no time to spend on daydreams. But she'd have to have been blind not to admire the fine-looking man who stood before her. Despite the fact that he had come, uninvited, into her home, at the sight of him she curtsied politely. And judging by the heat in her cheeks, she was blushing.

He noticed and responded with a knowing grin, stomping the ice from his boots and swinging his arms to force warmth to his hands. 'My dear, you are a sight for travel-weary eyes.' He spoke slowly and clearly, as though he suspected that she had not just ignored his knock, but truly could not hear. 'The roads are nothing but ruts from here to Oxford. I abandoned my carriage, stuck in the mud, and rode the rest of the way myself. But by God, I am here on time.' He reached into his pocket, withdrew a paper and slammed it down on the kitchen table. 'Go find Mr Marsh and tell him that the day is saved! The special licence has arrived. The wedding will go on as planned. Then get me a cup of mulled wine, or whatever passes for a holiday drink in these parts. I am frozen to the bone.' He dropped down into the best chair by the fire and removed his boots so that he might warm his feet.

For a moment, all about Generva seemed to freeze, as well. She could not decide what made her the most angry. Was it the demand for wine? To be mistaken for a servant in her own home? Or that the assumption came from this particularly attractive man? In the end, she decided it was the licence that most bothered her.

It was a pity. Until that moment, she had been managing to contain her emotions on the subject quite well. But to have the thing appear when she was holding a weapon…

Chapter Two

'What the devil?' It was all the Duke of Montford could manage to get out before the broom hit him a second time. He raised an arm to take the majority of the force, but the bristles still slapped sharply against the back of his head. The blow was surprisingly strong coming from such a petite woman.

'Take your licence back to your master and tell him what he can do with it,' she said, raising the broom again.

It was the last straw, a strangely appropriate metaphor given the instrument that struck him. 'I have no master other than the Regent.' He turned, stood and grabbed the broom handle on the next downswing. 'Now find Mr Marsh. I must speak with him.'

'I am *Mrs* Marsh,' she said in a glacial tone, not releasing her hold on the other end of the broom. 'State your business, sir.'

They stood for a moment, gazes locked. 'And I am the Duke of Montford. I have come with the special licence for my nephew's wedding.' He did not add, 'And put down the broom.' With the mention of his title, it should not have been necessary.

'You are not,' she said, with such conviction that he almost doubted his own identity. She kept a firm grip on her end of the handle. 'The duke is estranged from his nephew and was not expected here.'

Montford winced. It was perfectly true. But to hear it spoken as common knowledge was still painful. 'What better time than at a Christmas wedding to mend the relationship between myself and my heir?' It was one thing to maintain a cordial distance from young Tom and quite another to ignore his marriage. The boy was a blockhead for choosing to marry in the country at such an inappropriate time of year, of course. But when had he been anything but a blockhead? 'He asked for help with the licence. I obliged. Now I have come to meet the girl who will be the next duchess and give my good wishes.' If she was anything like her mother, she was comely enough. He must hope that she was better tempered.

'The next duchess?' Mrs Marsh smiled with incredulity. 'Then you will not be looking in this house, Your Grace. There will be no wedding. Now put on your boots and be on your way.' She released the broom and pointed a dire hand at the licence. 'And throw that thing into the fire.'

'I beg your pardon, madam.' He tugged on the broom again and delivered the words with the faintest hint of warning to remind her that this was no way to treat a peer.

'You heard me, unless you are as deaf as your nephew is dishonourable. Throw that thing into the fire and leave my house this instant.'

'I most certainly will not.' He grabbed the broom and threw it aside. 'I went to some trouble procuring it to allow for the Christmas Day wedding your daughter desired.'

'Well, you can *un*procure it. It is not needed. Take it to London, or take it to the devil for all I care. But it and you are not welcome in this house.'

What had Tom done now? When he had realised that he was likely to die childless, Montford had informed the young man of his future and offered advice and guidance. In response, his heir had announced that he was of age and past the point where he need seek approval of his decisions. He would do just as he pleased, now, and at such time as the title fell to him.

It was just what Montford feared most. He calmed himself, for there was no reason to fan the flames.

'Please, madam, enlighten me. Was there an estrangement of some kind that might still be mended?'

To this, she did nothing but laugh. 'Estrangement?
No, why should there be? Everything was as right as
rain until the third reading of the banns. There was a
disturbance in the church. An objection,' she said with
a dark look.

'Who could possibly object, if I did not?' he said,
equally surprised.

'You nephew's wife seemed to think she had the right,'
Mrs Marsh replied, wiping her hands upon her apron
as though she had touched something distasteful. 'His
Scottish wife. His pregnant Scottish wife. If you wish to
meet your next duchess, I suggest you go to Aberdeen.'

The duke dropped the broom and sat down in the
chair, for the moment as overwhelmed as the housewife.

She stood over him, clearly unwilling to give way. 'We
will have to return to that church on Christmas morning
for services. There will be no wedding, of course. Just
shame and embarrassment, and the gossip from the congregation. We are already the talk of the High Street. It
is likely to get much worse as more people learn of it.'
She waved an arm around the house. 'Here am I with the
larders full of dainties, a wedding cake already baked
and a daughter locked in her room who will not stop
weeping.'

It was worse than he could have imagined. He would

not reject a Scottish bride, or a child born barely to the right side of the blanket. But he could not allow the title to fall to a man who would flirt with bigamy as a solution to an awkward first marriage. 'And I suppose your daughter is compromised,' he said gloomily.

'How dare you, Your Grace.' Mrs Marsh grabbed for the broom again, and he snatched it out of her reach. 'Perhaps things are different in London, where chaperones are easily duped. But I know better than to allow my only daughter to be alone in the company of a gentleman, no matter how august his family connections. I did not allow so much as a kiss to pass between them.'

He held up the hand that did not already hold a broom. 'My apologies, my dear Mrs Marsh. My statement has more to do with my knowledge of my heir than your lovely daughter. The boy is a moron in most things, but can be sly when it is least convenient. I find it hard to believe that he did not at least attempt…'

'Of course he attempted,' she said with a frown. 'But I am a very light sleeper.' She looked significantly at the broom in his hand and smiled as though reliving a fond and violent memory.

'Very well, then.' He sighed with relief. 'All is not lost.'

'So you say,' she said with a huff. 'The truth will not matter, when all is said and done. Gentlemen of good family are unlikely to take my word for her virtue. What mother would not lie if she felt her daughter's happiness was at stake? They will assume the worst. No man will want her now that she is notorious.'

She was right, of course. It was a disaster for the Marsh family and a black mark on his own. A greater calamity lay ahead. Since he would be dead when his nephew took the coronet, there would be no way he could clean up the future messes that were made, as he would with this.

It was not fair. He thought of the row of graves in the family cemetery, two large and two small. He had vowed that there would be no third attempt to get a son of his own.

Now it seemed there was no choice.

When he spoke, it was slowly and with some care. 'I cannot mend a broken heart. But I think there is a solution that will solve all other problems to your satisfaction. If you would do me the honour of allowing me to pay court to your daughter, I will make an offer and marry her myself, assuming she is agreeable to it.'

Chapter Three

Generva sat on the bench opposite him and tried to catch her breath. His strange announcement took the air from her lungs as effectively as a blow from the broom. When she could gather her wits sufficiently to respond, she said, 'You cannot be serious.'

The duke gave her another thoughtful look. 'I do not see why not.'

'You have not even met the girl, for one thing.' While it would solve the problem of Gwen's reputation, total strangers did not simply step in and offer, as if they were helping the girl over a stile on the walk to church.

'But I am acquainted with her mother,' he said, smiling reasonably. 'A very limited acquaintance, perhaps.'

She shook her head, suddenly embarrassed. 'Striking you with a broom is hardly a proper introduction.'

'Then allow me.' He stood and bowed to her. 'I am Thomas Kanner, Duke of Montford.' He smiled again. 'There are other, lesser titles, of course. I'd have given one to young Tom on the occasion of his marriage. Your daughter would have been Lady Kanner.' The smile tightened. 'But under the circumstances, I think not.'

'But if she marries you, she will be…' Generva's breath caught in her lungs again.

'The Duchess of Montford.' He was helping again. She imagined his arm at her elbow, lifting her over the stile.

'Duchess of Montford,' she repeated. It was a coup. Everything that a mother could wish for her daughter. Why was she not instantly happy at the thought?

'Now that we are likely to be family, I see no reason that you might not call me Thomas, Mrs Marsh.'

There was one very obvious reason. She could not dare call him Thomas because he was the Duke of Montford. She was just getting used to the fact that she would call him His Grace. She had never met a duke, nor had she expected to. When Tom Kanner had begun to pay court on Gwen, he had made it clear that his most important relative was both distant and disapproving. They communicated in writing, if at all. When the Marshes finally saw the great man, it was likely to be at his funeral, after Tom had taken the title for himself.

Now here he was in her kitchen, with a broom straw still stuck in his hair from the assault she had waged on his person.

'Mrs Marsh?' he said, leaning a little closer to her. He waved a hand in front of her eyes, as though attempting to wake her from a trance.

'You may call me Generva,' she said weakly.

'That is a lovely name,' he replied. 'As is—' he shot a surreptitious glance at the special licence on the table '—Gwendolyn.'

She started. A licence. 'You would need to go back to London for another licence. Or wait the three weeks to have the banns read...'

'We could simply use this one.' He pushed the paper towards her. 'My nephew and I share a name.' He glanced at the paper. 'My title is not on the licence, of course. But there is some space left on the line. I will take up a quill, wedge it in the gap and sign properly at the bottom. Then the wedding can go on, just as planned.'

'That could not be legal,' Generva said with a frown.

'If propriety concerns you, I will sleep at the inn until such a time as we can travel down to London and procure another licence. We will marry again, quietly, in the new year.'

'At the Fox's Tail? Oh, dear Lord, no, Your Grace. That would not do.'

He gave her a surprised look. 'I assure you, madam,

I am not so high and mighty that I cannot take a room there, with the rest of the common travellers.

'Fleas,' she said, in an embarrassed whisper. 'We locals call the place the Dog's Hind Leg. You can spot the guests in the street for the way they scratch.'

'Thank you for your warning, Generva.'

Her given name was probably meant as a reminder that they were to be on friendly terms.

'You're welcome, Thomas.' His name escaped her lips as a hoarse croak. 'And you are welcome here. You will take the best bed in the house for the duration of your stay.' That was her bed, she supposed. She could share with Gwendolyn, which was probably the best. She would be there as chaperone.

Not that a chaperone was likely needed when the potential groom had such good manners and the bride to be could not stop crying over another man.

'Certainly not.' The duke's voice cut through the wool in her head. 'You are thinking of displacing yourself, are you not? I will not hear of that. Any place will do. A rug by the fire, perhaps—'

The conversation was interrupted by the creaking of the pantry door and the appearance of a single grubby hand, fumbling for another of the pies on the table.

Generva was on her feet in a moment to seize the boy by the wrist to haul him into the room. 'Your Grace, may I introduce my other child, Benjamin Marsh.' She gave one quick glance to his face, relieved that there were not too many smudges upon it, and gave a half-hearted swipe with her fingers to straighten his hair, before turning him to face their guest. 'Benjamin, offer your greetings to His Grace the Duke of Montford.' When Benjamin seemed frozen in place, she pushed gently on his back to encourage the bow.

The duke gave him a sombre look. 'I have been sent by the Regent to look into the local theft of mince pies.'

The boy shot a horrified look to the crumbling crust in his hand.

Then the duke laughed heartily and stepped forward to take the cleaner of the two small hands. 'I am sorry, I could not resist.' He glanced down at Benjamin. 'I am Tom Kanner's uncle, come for the wedding.' He glanced at Generva. 'I will happily displace this boy from his bed. I suspect he deserves a night on the floor for something he has done recently.'

'Fair enough.' Generva smiled back. 'Benjamin, go prepare your room for a guest.'

When the boy had taken the back stairs to the first floor, they were alone again. She felt the room growing more sombre by the minute as the enormity of what was occurring came home to her. To hide her confusion, she prepared the drink that the duke had requested, setting a mug of brandy and hot water on the table beside his hand. 'Now, about your kind offer…'

He gave her a sad smile. 'That was almost delivered in a tone of refusal, Mrs Marsh.'

She thought for a moment and poured a drink for herself, returning to the bench opposite. 'What kind of a mother would I be to accept for her with no thought at all?' She would be a very sensible one. She could not think of a better answer to the dilemma. But somehow she could not manage the heartfelt thanks he deserved. Instead, she whispered, 'You would do that for her? You would marry a girl you had never seen to save her from disgrace?'

'It is not solely for her,' the duke said with a sigh. 'With each passing year, it grows more apparent that I cannot trust my title and holdings to the man who will inherit them. As much as it goes against my wishes to marry again, I must attempt it.' At last, she noticed the little lines of strain around the smile and the creases at the corners of his eyes that had not all been caused by mirth.

'You do not wish to marry, Your Grace?' When speaking for her daughter, it would be easier to respect his title and not foster this closeness that seemed to grow so quickly between them. 'Then why do it? And to a stranger?' She was tempted to add that the girl he was planning to wed was much younger than he was and hardly old enough to know her own mind on the subject of love and matrimony. But she had been younger still when she had married John. He had been a good fifteen years her senior and she had been most happy in the union.

Her prospective son-in-law was nearly the same age as her husband had been and staring mournfully into his cup. 'I have been married twice before, Generva. Each time I have taken the time to know my bride and her family. If the matches were not the love stories of an age, I can assure you that they were sweet enough to satisfy.' He took a drink. 'I did not plan to lose a wife to childbirth. It hurt even more the second time.' He took another sip, his smile totally gone. 'There is a limit to what the human heart can endure, Mrs Marsh. I had no desire to tempt fate a third time. But it seems, if only for the sake of Montford's future tenants, I must do something.'

How had she not noticed what was hidden behind his earlier smiles? She knew that sorrow, for she carried it with her. It had been five years since the horrible letter arrived, explaining that she would never see her beloved again. It was like an old scar that still ached. She could not help herself, but reached out and covered the duke's hand with her own.

The moment she touched him, she wished that she had not. If things went as they were planning, it would not be her place to comfort him, it would be Gwendolyn's.

He did not seem to notice, clasping her hand in gratitude. There was a deep sigh, then his smile returned. 'If something must be done, it is probably better that it is done quickly. And I would prefer a girl who is strong and healthy to one who is lovely but delicate. Perhaps mutual gratitude and respect will be a more enduring foundation than the tender emotions of my youth.'

She wanted to argue that his youth was not yet gone, any more than hers was. They were not children anymore, but she had seen first fatherhood come to older men than Montford. And there were several women her age in the village still carrying babes in their bellies or their arms.

There was a strange burning in her throat as she swallowed the words of comfort. It was probably deserved indigestion from taking brandy so early in the day. Anything else—jealousy or regret, for example—would be most unworthy of her. He might be old enough to start again. But in the years that she had been alone, no gentlemen had shown interest, nor did she expect a change in her circumstances. She must learn to accept that that part of her life was over.

But Gwen's life was just beginning. Generva would not be upset. She was grateful, just as a good mother should be. Now she must tell him so. 'That is very generous of you,' she said, trying to look as happy as she should by the offer. 'I cannot speak for Gwendolyn, of course. But I give you my permission to speak to her

on the subject. Your room will be the one at the head of
the stairs. Please, go and refresh yourself. I will tell my
daughter the good news.'

Chapter Four

As he walked up the stairs, Montford whistled a few bars of 'The Coventry Carol', then thought the better of it. The song was beautiful, but melancholy. If he was serious about becoming a bridegroom, he would do well to put sad thoughts aside.

At the very least, he could learn to laugh at his own foolishness for suggesting such a thing. At his age, he should know better than to speak without thinking of the potential consequences. He had no proof that he would be able to stand the sight of the girl, much less bed her. Nor did he know if the girl would make a suitable duchess.

Of course, he had irrefutable proof that young Tom would make a terrible Montford. He must trust that

Gwendolyn took after her mother both in looks and sensibility. If she did, all would be well. The mother had hair the colour of nutmeg without a strand of grey in it, and a piquant temper, as well. After two children, her figure was still trim. Her cheeks were rosy from the cold, but their skin was smooth and unblemished. She'd have been prettier had she smiled, of course. But she'd had little reason to do so.

All in all, she was a most handsome woman. After dinner tonight, he would offer the as-yet-unseen Mr Marsh his congratulations on his own fortunate marriage.

But now he'd arrived at the door to his temporary chamber and was greeted by a probing look from the recalcitrant Benjamin. He dropped the small bag of clothing he had brought with him on a chair beside the bed and met the boy's gaze. 'We meet again, Master Marsh. I wish to wash before dinner.' He glanced at the boy's grimy hands. 'You should, as well. Is there water to be had in this room, or must I go back to the kitchen?'

The boy pointed to the pitcher and basin in the corner.

Montford poured out a generous amount and began to splash the road dirt from his face and hands.

He could feel the gaze of the boy, heavy on the back of his neck. 'So you are a duke.' The boy spoke as if the fact was somehow in doubt.

Montford gave a slight bow of his head in acknowledgement, but did not turn around. 'Indeed I am.'

'You don't look like a duke.'

'And how is a duke supposed to appear?'

'Well, you wouldn't be in Reddington, for one thing. We see the squire in church sometimes. But no dukes.' The boy said it with a finality that suggested he was unsure of the existence of the peerage as a species.

'I came here for the wedding,' Montford reminded him. 'My nephew was to marry your sister. If you have seen him, you have seen the heir to a dukedom. It is very nearly the same thing.'

'So he said,' the boy replied. 'But if that is any indication of what dukes are like, I've had enough of them, and good riddance.'

Montford dried his face and went to sit down on the bed beside him. 'Unfortunately, he is not a very good example. His behaviour was most ignoble.'

The boy nodded. 'She is better off without him. When he met me, he handed me the reins to his horse without so much as a please or thank-you.' The eyes narrowed again. 'And he patted my head.'

'He did not dare,' the duke said, trying to sound indignant.

'But he did not pat Boney.' When he saw the duke's confusion, he added. 'Our spaniel. He is the best dog in the world.'

'I saw him at the door,' the duke agreed. 'He does appear to be a most devoted animal.'

'Tom Kanner walked by him as though he was not even there,' the boy said with a frown. 'And when Boney got in the way, he kicked him.'

'He did not,' the duke said, actually indignant this time.

'He moved him with his boot,' the boy amended. 'But if he will not treat a dog properly, it was no surprise that he was not right to my sister.'

'That is a most wise assessment,' the duke agreed. 'I am afraid I must agree with you. Young Tom is a blight on the family tree. He paid no attention to his father when that man was alive. Now that he thinks he will have my coronet, he pays no attention to me, either.' Montford tried not to frown as he said it. How wise was it, really, to tell his greatest worry to a ten-year-old boy? 'In any case, I should not have mentioned him. He is nothing like a duke at all. You must not judge me based on your acquaintance with him.'

'So long as you do not kick my dog, I shall not,' the boy said, though he was clearly not impressed. Then he asked, with no preamble, 'Have you met Lord Nelson?'

'Unfortunately, I have not.'

Benjamin gave a disapproving shake of his head, and Montford could tell that he had fallen one notch further down the ladder of approval.

'But I have met the king,' he added, to save face. 'The Regent, as well. And Wellington, of course,' he added, for what little boy was not eager to hear of him?

Apparently this one. 'My father was in the navy,' he said, as though that settled the matter. 'He was the captain of a ship. He is dead now.'

The news hit him with the force of a broom. *Dead?* It made sense, of course. The lovely Generva Marsh certainly behaved as though she was master as well as mistress of the house. Her husband must have been gone for some time. There was no sign of mourning in her clothing or behaviour.

Unless one counted the way she had taken his hand as he'd talked of his own troubles. Despite the fact that he had just offered for young Gwendolyn, he had been quite envious of Captain Marsh at that moment. But if Captain Marsh existed only in memory…

It was too late to have such thoughts. He had just asked permission to court her daughter. If only he'd known that the fearless creature who had taken a broom to him was widowed… One wondered what she might strike him with should he announce that he had mistakenly offered for the wrong woman.

'Even if you have met King George, it does not mean that I need give you my bed, despite what my mother might think.' Master Marsh was a sensible creature, more concerned with his own comfort than making nice to strangers for the sake of their titles.

'I will play you for it,' the duke said. 'We could match coins.'

'Do I get to keep the coin if I win?' the boy asked.

'Not if you wish to keep the bed, as well,' the duke said.

'Very well.' The boy nodded. 'Then give me the coin and you can have the bed. But do not tell my mother about it. She would not approve.'

With the arrival of the duke, dinner became another source of stress. When Generva had awoken, she'd planned for nothing more than a simple meal. It was still a day from Christmas Eve, not yet even part of the twelve-day celebration that the duke's household probably made of Christmas. With the departure of Tom Kanner, her own house was practically in mourning.

Suddenly, she found herself entertaining the peerage. She had never played hostess to a man of such rank. Indeed, the most exciting invitation she had received was for a single dinner in the house of the local baron, and that had been as an honour to her husband. They had been seated nowhere near the head of the table. The food had been grand enough, though, and tonight she would have to struggle to emulate it.

With a sigh, she ordered Mrs Jordan to cook the roast

that had been set aside for Christmas dinner, as many side dishes as could be found in the pantry, and for her to take more than usual care not to burn the potatoes. She could open the bottle of wine that she had been saving as a gift for the happy couple. Her favourite apple tart was really quite simple, but would look better if the crust was dressed with an arrangement of sugar leaves and apples. And there would be the last of her husband's port for after.

With the supper menu settled, she went upstairs to the bedrooms to roust her erstwhile children so that they might know what was expected of them.

First she rapped sharply on Gwen's door and informed her through the panel that there would be no more sulking or tears. If she did not open immediately, the door would be broken down and she would be hauled out by the hair. Once the girl had grudgingly given her permission to enter, Generva informed her of the events of the afternoon, the recent change of fortune and the duke's generous offer.

Her daughter's response was as she feared it would be. 'Absolutely not!'

Generva took a deep breath, and proceeded with caution. 'But, darling, you must at least come out of your room and thank the man for his kindness. Think of the honour he pays you in making this offer at all.'

'I would rather not think of it,' her daughter said, wip-

ing at her tear-swollen eyes. 'I do not want a thing from
Tom Kanner or his family. I especially do not want to
see anyone associated with him ever again.'

In that she could hardly be blamed. It still did not
give her the right to be discourteous. 'I understand you
are hurt. But you must realise that the cancellation of
the wedding will leave us both in a difficult position.'

'Because I am now cast-off goods, known as a fool
in front of the entire church?' Gwen's voice was growing shrill. 'That is no fault of mine.'

'Of course not, dear.' Generva bit her lip to remember
the need for patience. 'But if you meet him, you will see
that the Duke of Montford is quite different from Tom.'

'Because he is old enough to be my father.'

Almost exactly old enough, which was something
Generva preferred not to think about. 'That does not
mean he is ancient. If you meet him, you will find him
kind and sensible in ways that a younger man is not.
He has an excellent temper, and is very handsome for a
man of his years.

She glanced past her daughter at her own reflection
in the mirror above the dresser. What did it say about
the state of her looks that the most handsome man she
had seen in ages immediately assumed that she was
a housekeeper? It did not matter, really. She was long
past the point where vanity ruled her feelings. Nor was

there any reason to put on airs in hopes of attracting a new husband.

All the same, it rankled. She tugged at the cap on her head, making an effort to tuck the curls around it in a more becoming way.

'If you think he is such a prize, then perhaps you should be the one to marry him.' Gwendolyn threw herself back on to the bed again, as though preparing for another bout of weeping.

'He did not offer to marry me,' Generva said, struggling and failing to hide the bitterness in her voice. 'And I am not the one who needs a husband. I had one. Since no one is likely to appear at the back door with a proposal, I have learned to manage without.' She immediately regretted the outburst. It had been a difficult week for all of them, but it had been worst for Gwen. She needed a mother who would be kind to her. Generva had failed, utterly.

But perhaps a little cruelty had been needed. The sharpness in her tone was as effective as a slap to her daughter's face. The girl sat up, staring at her in alarm, and wiped the tears from her eyes as if to get a clearer view of her own mother.

Generva took another breath and was back in control again. 'I have no intention of forcing you into a marriage you do not want. But you must come down to dinner and meet the man to thank him for his concern.

Perhaps you will feel different at the end of the evening. Perhaps not. But you must not shed another tear over a man who has proved unworthy. Now wash your face and put on your best dress. Tonight you will dine with the Duke of Montford.'

From there, she went to Benjamin's room, relieved to see that the duke was absent from it. But her son remained, and she dragged him to the basin and scrubbed the boy within an inch of his life before forcing him into his best suit.

'I do not see why we must wash, Mama,' he said. 'The duke has seen me dirty already.'

She gritted her teeth and ran a comb through the boy's tangle of straw-coloured hair. 'And now he shall see you clean, for the sake of your mother's pride, if for no other reason. The man is a peer, not a greengrocer. I cannot have your dirty neck spoiling his appetite for supper.'

'He has said I may call him old Tom.'

Generva flinched. 'Well, I say you may not. You will call him Your Grace, and bow when you meet him, just as you would when meeting the vicar.'

'I do not like the vicar,' Benjamin announced.

'Well, do you like the duke?'

The boy thought for a moment. 'I think so.'

'Then bow,' she said, giving another tug on his hair.

From outside the bedroom door, she was convinced she heard a deep, masculine chuckle.

* * *

A short time later, they were gathered round the table, the meat steaming on a platter in front of them. The scene was a perfect picture of domestic bliss. Or it would have been, had not Gwen been sagging in her chair like a drowned Ophelia, her face wan, her eyes red rimmed and her shoulders drooping.

It was all Generva could do to keep from kicking her under the table.

The duke seemed to take no notice of the girl's unwelcoming posture and smiled from the head of the table. 'May I offer the blessing?' he asked.

'Of course,' she murmured, surprised that he seemed so eager.

After a moment's thoughtful silence, he began to sing. 'Come, let us join our cheerful songs with angels round the throne…'

She had known his singing voice was lovely, but nothing she had heard thus far compared to this. For the brief space of the hymn, even Benjamin was spellbound and Gwen's frown replaced with awe.

Then, as though nothing unusual had happened, the duke reached for the platter and helped himself to a large slice of beef.

When Generva could find her breath again, she said with sincerity, 'You have a beautiful voice, Your Grace.' The compliment hardly did it justice. The hairs on the back of her neck were still standing in awareness of the rumbling basso.

He gave a shrug and a smile. 'I had little choice in the matter. My mother was a Wesleyan, you see. She sang morning and night. My father was a different sort.' His smile broadened at the memory. 'There is a Christmas tradition, in our holdings, that the lord of the manor should be able to match mummers and wassailers verse for verse to make them earn the cup they are begging for.' He was positively grinning. 'I have upheld it, as well. They will miss me this week, I'm sure, for we have a fine time of it.'

'I like the song about the dead boar better,' Benjamin said with a firm nod. 'The one you sang to me in my room.'

'The boar's head in hand bear I, bedecked with bay and rosemary.' Montford thundered out the first line as though there were nothing unusual about singing during dinner. 'I shall teach it to you later, if your mother allows it. I suspect you have a fine singing voice.'

He turned his attention to Gwen, trying to draw her into the conversation. 'And you, my dear. Do you sing, as well?'

Generva leaned forward, all but crossing her fingers under the table.

Her daughter gave an indifferent shrug. 'I have little reason to sing.'

Damn the girl for being such a wet hen. Desperate to keep the conversation going, Generva spoke for her. 'She is simply being modest. Gwen has a lovely soprano tone and has, on occasion, sung solos in our church.'

The girl's eyes rose to meet her, in shock at the bald-faced lie. Their vicar, the Reverend Mr Allcot, had strong opinions concerning Methodists and their desire to turn the church into what he deemed little better than a Covent Garden music hall. He preferred rites celebrated in respectful silence, or with a minimum of plain song. He'd have resigned his living before allowing a soprano soloist.

The duke nodded sagely as though he could think of nothing better. Then he turned to her. 'I am sure it is a perfect match for your voice, which is deeper.'

'How would you know?' It was true, of course. But she'd had no idea that he had noticed anything about her, much less the timbre of her voice.

'You were humming in the kitchen just a while ago. And as you combed your son's hair.' He smiled fondly at her. 'You have a fine voice. I do not suppose you have a pianoforte or a spinet?'

'I am sorry, Your Grace, but no.' It was not precisely too dear for the budget, but she had not thought, since John had died, to spend on such an extravagance.

'A pity. I suspect that we would sing quite nicely together, should we attempt it.'

He must mean the four of them. What else could he mean? But for a brief, irrational moment, she imagined a duet. What was it about the man that made her so foolish? There was nothing in his manner or his words that was provocative, but she could not seem to stop seeking a hidden meaning in them.

It was a good thing that he would be gone in a day or two. If Gwen rebuffed his offer, what reason would he have to remain? And if he did, what was she to feed him? He had demolished the better part of the roast and taken a second helping of the tart, as well. She was unused to a having a man with a hearty appetite under her roof.

Her thoughts strayed back to appetites of a different sort and she stifled them behind a tight, hospitable smile. 'But tonight you are likely too tired after your long ride to visit us.'

He smiled back at her, in no way encumbered by dark thoughts. 'Not so very tired that I would not enjoy the port I see on the sideboard and some conversation before the fire in the parlour,' he said.

Here was another problem. 'I am sorry, Your Grace. Of late, we've had to retire early because of the cold. We cannot seem to get the chimney in the parlour to draw. Until I can find a man from the village to see to it…'

He stood and spread his arms wide. 'You have a man here, Mrs Marsh. Let us go and have a look.'

'But, Your Grace…' At moments like this, there was

nothing genteel about the poverty they lived in. It was humiliating. And it made her fantasies about the duke all the more ridiculous.

But again, he did not seem bothered by their circumstances. 'Please, I will hear no spurious arguments about my rank, my dear Mrs Marsh. What sort of gentleman would I be if I did not offer aid to a lady in distress? Lead me to the problem and I shall endeavour to fix it.'

As Mrs Jordan hurried ahead of them with a taper, the family retired to their best room, which was dark despite being in the centre of the house. Once lit, it was cheerful enough, but unwelcoming because of the cold. Thank the Lord and the housekeeper that the hearth was clean. The Duke of Montford was on his knees in an instant, strong body half inside the fireplace, his head disappearing up the chimney. A hand appeared, waving a vague gesture into the room. Then came his deep voice, amplified by the chimney. 'Hold the candle close, boy. I can almost see the problem, but I need more light.'

For once, Benjamin did as he was told and stood like a loyal squire, holding the light and passing the poker that was requested as Montford mumbled about a stuck flue.

The women held their breath.

There was a screech of rusted metal, a satisfying *thunk* and a trickle of soot as the flue returned to its proper setting.

'There.' Montford backed out of the opening, replac-

ing the poker in the rack and reaching for a handkerchief
to wipe his hands and knees. 'We will have a fire laid
in no time and the room shall be warm as toast. It was
a simple thing to remedy. It needed only a long arm and
a moderate amount of muscle....'

And then, Benjamin's good behaviour, which was a
precarious thing at best, collapsed under a temptation
too great to ignore. He kicked the kneeling peer in the
seat of his breeches and shouted, 'Hot cockles!'

The poor man started forward, banging his head into
the brick. Another shower of soot fell from above, dark-
ening his face and shoulders.

To compound Generva's mortification, her beautiful
daughter, who had been weeping steadily for a week,
took one look at the situation and stifled a giggle. And
then another. If she was not removed from the room immediately, they might grow from titters to laughs and
sink them all.

'Go,' Generva said, in an angry whisper that seemed
to fill the room. 'Go! Both of you.' She glared at Gwen.
'Put him to bed and then go back to your room. Or I
swear...'

From the floor behind her came a congenial call of,
'Goodnight, Miss Marsh. And you as well, you snot-
nosed ruffian. I will deal with you later.'

Chapter Five

In Montford's opinion, there was nothing quite like a social disaster to guarantee a pleasant evening. In an effort to please him, the hostess's nerves were usually strung as tightly as the wires on a pianoforte. Just as Generva Marsh had been when they'd been at table.

The food had been excellent. The children had been clean and polite. The lady of the house had taken extra care with her own *toilette* and donned a gown of burgundy satin, cut low enough to show the freckles on her shoulders and bosom and to leave her shivering in the chill air of the dining room. Was any room but the kitchen ever truly warm in December?

She had dressed her hair as well, with worked gold pins that were probably the pride of a limited jewellery box. Captain Marsh had been a loving husband, but unsuccessful in taking prizes, if this was all he could manage for those dark brown curls.

It was a joy to look at her. But it seemed that would be the only pleasure of the evening. The conversation was stilted and dull. Master Ben was presented with a heaping plate so that he might be too busy to speak wrong. And it was clear, from her wary eyes and stubborn chin, that Miss Marsh was not the least bit interested in his solution to her disgrace. Out of courtesy, he had done his best to engage her in conversation and she had resisted at every turn.

It was just as well. If she changed her mind tomorrow, he'd have to keep his word and marry her. But when he looked at her, he felt nothing more than polite curiosity. It did not bode well for a possible marriage between them.

Especially since he could not seem to stop staring at her mother. Generva was not a memorable beauty, as his first wife had been, but she was quite lovely. Nor was she as witty as his second wife, though she was more than clever enough to suit him. More important, she had suffered both pain and hardship and was still very much alive. Wit and beauty had been transient things when compared with the rigours of childbirth. But Generva had faced them twice already and survived. In fact, she seemed to have thrived.

And now that all hell had broken loose in the parlour, he would have her all to himself.

She shooed the children away, then handed him a blanket for his shoulders and insisted that he remove his coat so that the housekeeper could brush the coal dust from it before it was ruined.

He kept it long enough to lay a fire for them, then did as he was bidden. By the whispering of the two women, it was only propriety that kept them from demanding he surrender his breeches for cleaning, as well. They would likely disappear in the night and be clean in the morning, just as the coat had when the housekeeper left.

'I am sorry.' The words were out of Generva's mouth before the door could latch.

Generva. It was a fine name. He looked forward to using it often, rolling it around in his mouth like a fine wine. 'You have nothing to apologise for.'

'My family behaved disgracefully.' She was not wringing her hands, as some women might, but stood tall, like a young officer on the deck of her husband's ship, waiting to be dressed down.

'All families do, at one time or other. It is my nephew's terrible behaviour that brought me to you.' He fumbled in his pocket for a handkerchief.

'At least he did not kick anyone in the ar—the bottom,' she amended. 'Here. Allow me.' She pushed him towards a seat by the fire and took the handkerchief from him, dabbing carefully at his face.

He watched intently as she perched on the arm of the sofa and dipped the corner of it into her mouth, then wiped at the soot on his face. Did she mean to clean him like a cat with a kitten?

Because he would not mind that.

'Ben grows worse each year,' she admitted quietly as she worked.

'He will grow worse until he grows better,' the duke agreed. 'All boys his age are monsters. The trick he played on me was but a child's game. I played it myself, when at school. One boy must put on a blindfold. One of the others hits him and shouts, "Hot cockles". Then the victim must guess the assailant.'

'There was only one possible assailant,' she said with a dark look towards the upper floor.

'It did take the mystery from it,' he agreed. 'But my posture was all but asking for a kick. At that age, my mother would have needed to physically restrain me from taking action.'

'It is proof of what idiots men can be when there are no women around to stop them from it.' She switched the dirty linen in her hand for her own handkerchief and dipped it in the water from a drinking glass set beside his port. 'Or perhaps it is that he needs a father. I worry, when he is old enough, he will run away to join the navy.'

Her hand stilled in her lap. Either he was clean to her satisfaction, or the thought of losing another man to the sea distressed her.

'Do you mean to find him one?'

Her distant look turned to one of confusion.

'A father,' he said carefully. 'Do you mean to find a husband? You are still young enough to remarry.'

But too old to blush over it, apparently. There was no pink in her cheek, other than what had been there from the first. He would not have compared her face to porcelain, unless it was to note the contrast of pale-pink rose petals painted on china. 'A lady does not get herself a husband,' she informed him. 'A lady waits until a gentleman makes up his mind.' She smiled. 'And this lady has reconciled herself to the fact that none is coming.'

He took a sip of the port, which was excellent. It appeared that Captain Marsh had had excellent taste, all around. 'Courting is not as I remember it. I thought I was the quarry, not the hunter.'

'Because you are titled, Your Grace,' she said with a smile that was much less sad. 'I am a widow. Should I be the pursuer, society will think I am searching for something far different than a father for my children.'

Might she be longing for companionship? Did she miss a man in her bed? Or was that just what men wished to think, so that they need not worry about the reputation of the widows they claimed to be protecting? 'I hope my presence here does not lead to more gossip,' he said. 'When I arrived, I assumed there was a man of the house. Now it is evening and we are unchaperoned.'

She laughed, and it was a sweet sound, as youthful as her daughter's face. 'If anyone talks, I will inform them that you are a duke and ask them if they thought you rode all the way from London because you had heard of my beauty. Then I will remind them of the fleas at the inn. If I could think of a house that was not already too full to hold you, I might have sent you there. But I could not.'

'As long as I am no trouble,' he said.

'It is only for a few nights.' Then she remembered their original plan. 'And I wished for you to meet my daughter.'

Should he tell her now of the hopelessness of that particular plan? Better to wait until he could offer another. Though one was already forming in his mind, he had no evidence that she would approve of it. 'Your daughter. Ah. Yes. Gwendolyn is a lovely girl. I suspect I will have a chance to talk to her again tomorrow. But tonight, I will retire early. If you will excuse me, Mrs Marsh?'

'Of course, Your Grace.' She hopped from her perch on the arm of the sofa and offered him a candle to light the way to his room.

Once there, he found the boy sound asleep on the far

edge of the mattress. Boney, the spaniel, was monopolising the hot bricks that had been tucked under the sheets to warm their feet. He had a good mind to wake the boy and demand his penny back. He had bought the rights to the bed that afternoon.

But on feeling the cold of the floor through his stockinged feet as he undressed for bed, he could not find it in his heart to displace the child. Instead, he pulled back the covers, climbed into the space remaining and tried to sleep.

Chapter Six

It came as some relief that the duke was an early riser on Christmas Eve morning and willing to partake of the breakfast Generva had ordered for the rest of the family. Only Gwen was absent. No amount of prodding could convince the ungrateful girl to leave her bed and take another meal with the duke.

For some reason, Generva could not manage to be as disappointed as she ought to be at the utter failure of his suit. A match with a duke should have been an answer to a mother's prayers. But she had not been looking forward to calling this particular man son-in-law. It would spoil some part of the friendship that had sprung up between them once she had set down the broom.

She smiled at the memory of their meeting.

The duke paused midbite to stare at her. 'At last the sun has come up, for Mrs Marsh is smiling. What are you plotting? Some surprise for Christmas, perhaps?'

Christmas. In the fuss over the wedding, she had forgotten to treat it as a holiday in its own right. She would have to find some nuts and an orange for Ben, and perhaps a few pennies. He must think he had been forgotten in the rush to marry off his sister. 'No surprise,' she admitted. 'It will not be as merry as some holidays we have shared. But we will manage.'

'I noticed the lack in your decorating thus far, madam.' He glanced at the bare mantel over the fireplace.

'Perhaps it is because in the country we cannot afford the extravagances of a ducal manor, Your Grace.' It was wrong to snap at him. It cost nothing to pull down some ivy from a nearby wood. She had been remiss.

'No worries,' he said with a smile. 'Ben and I will handle it all. The weather is fine and I fancy a walk after breakfast. We will return to green the house. And if it is not too early to do so, we might hunt a wren for St Stephen's Day.'

At this suggestion, her son's eyes brightened and he began shovelling kippers into his mouth as though fearing the duke might leave without him, should he linger too long at table.

Generva gave him a worried look. 'I shall only permit it if you promise me that no harm shall come to the bird. It is one thing to carry it alive from house to house. But to call it the king of all birds only to beg pennies for the burial of its poor little corpse, when it has done no harm to anyone…'

The duke laid a hand on her arm to calm her. 'I promise we shall build him a little cage and let him go when we are done.'

'Very well, then.' She gave him an approving nod. 'My son is quite bloodthirsty enough without encouragement.' The duke was saying *we* as though he meant to be here for the twenty-sixth to take the boy house to house himself. She could not exactly send the man away. But if there was no hope for a match with Gwen, how long did he mean to stay?

'Very well, then.' The duke was staring at the little boy across the table from him. 'Finish your breakfast. Then we will cut down some greens and harass the wildlife.'

It was only a moment more and Ben was pushing away from the table to search for a muffler and gloves. The duke took another sip of his coffee, then smiled at her and rose, bowing in her direction. 'Madam, if you will excuse me? Duty calls.'

She managed to contain her amazement until he had cleared the doorway. Was it fair that the man should be gallant, good-looking and willing to escort her fractious son into the woods? Ben liked him, as well. Not enough to cease playing pranks on him, of course. But Montford's amused response to them made him seem all the more attractive.

Thomas, she reminded herself. He had given her permission to use the name.

Then she remembered why she should not. A duke arriving at Christmas to marry her daughter was something straight out of a fairy tale. But in those stories, peers never appeared on the doorstep ready to set their titles aside so that they might be a father to young boys and rescue matrons from their lonely widowhood. Generva had never been fair, could hardly be called young and had not been a maiden for quite some time.

She must not forget, even for an instant, that her story had ended, unhappily, when John had died. In whatever plot continued, she was a minor character at best. Even the Duke of Montford was but a player in a single, short scene. She would force Gwen to meet with him this very day. If the girl did not want him, she must say so to his face. Then they might get him out of this house and on the road back to London. If not, she would be as foolish as her own daughter by Twelfth Night, weeping and mooning over a man she could not have.

'Holly and his merry men, they dance and they sing.' It was mid-afternoon before Montford's voice rang out in the front hall. Generva could feel the blast of air that had entered with him all the way to the back of the house.

'Ivy and her maidens, they weep and they wring.' She answered with the next line of the song almost before she could help herself. How annoyingly appropriate for the state of the house lately. She straightened her skirts and went to meet him. 'Close the door,' she called. 'You are letting in a draught.' Then she bit her tongue. Had she forgotten so quickly her plan to treat him as an honoured guest and not a member of the family who could be scolded and ordered about?

Her words did not seem to bother him. As she entered the hall, he was dragging the door shut with his foot, since his hands were too busy to do the task. He was carrying the plants he sang about, and pine boughs and mistletoe, as well. Ben was a step ahead of him, carrying a wooden cage with a small, unhappy bird hopping about inside.

'Have you cut down the whole forest and brought it into my house?' She had decorated in the past. But she had never needed such a profusion of greenery.

The duke responded to her frown with an innocent, almost boyish look. 'They will grow back, you know. Your mantel has no garland. Nor does your banister. If I mean to remedy the fact, I decided it was better to have too much than too little. I would not want to make a second trip.

'True,' she said, and took a deep breath. He had brought the scent of pine and fresh air into the house when he'd returned to it. Surely that explained the sudden buoyancy of her spirit.

'If you give me some twine, or perhaps a bit of wire, I shall set it all to rights.'

Would that you could. For a moment, the solid maleness of his voice washed her worries away. She did so miss having a helpmate. Not that John had been that much help, if she was honest. He was away far too often. She shook her head, as though trying to clear it, and said, 'It is my duty. You are a guest.'

'And I owe you much,' he said softly. 'It is better, staying here, than at the inn I would have chosen. But I have placed an unexpected burden of hospitality upon you.' He smiled in a way that was far too open and friendly for so important a man. 'It would be my pleasure to help you in this.'

She gave a little flutter of her hands, trying not to look as foolish as his words made her feel. 'Very well, then. I shall get the twine.' She was back in a moment with a work basket that held wire, hammer and nails, as well. At the last minute, she'd added a handful of bright red ribbons that she'd meant to save for trimming her wedding bonnet.

He nodded in approval and set to work. For a gentleman, he was surprisingly adept at it, twining the branches together and threading sprigs of holly through the wires. Ben had disappeared into the kitchen to find crumbs for his feathered prisoner, which left Generva to steady the branches and snip the wires that he tied. In no time at all, he'd fashioned a creditable swag and draped the banister with it.

He stood back satisfied. She had to admit, the results were impressive and the time expended had been minimal. They moved on to the parlour, piling the mantel with holly and ivy.

He glanced down at her. 'You are smiling again, Mrs Marsh. Twice in one day. It must truly be Christmas.'

Was it really so rare a thing to see her smile? She hoped not. But now that he had commented on it, she could not manage to raise the corners of her lips to prove him wrong.

The duke sighed. 'And now it is gone again. Do you think, if we put up a kissing bough, it will come back?'

'Certainly not.' At least he had given her a reason to frown. All the kindness in the world did not give him the right to tease her.

'You have several fine arches and a hook in the centre of the parlour where you might hang it.' He glanced up in mock sadness at the empty door frames. 'And yet, I see none there.'

'That is because there is no point in hanging something of that kind in this house,' she said firmly, as though the matter was settled. 'There is no one here that wants or needs kissing.'

'Really,' he said, surprised.

'My son is too young to care. If I allow my daughter to run riot at the holidays I will have even more trouble than I do already. The servants have no right to be distracted with it for half the month of December.'

'And you?' he prompted.

'I?' She did her best to pretend that the thought had not occurred to her. She turned away. 'It is foolishness, and I have no time for that, either.'

'Perhaps it is time to make the time,' he said, stepping forward, holding the branch above her head and kissing her on the lips before she could object.

It was as if the world had been spinning at a mad rate and suddenly stopped, leaving her vision unnaturally clear. She was not a minor character waiting in the wings of her own life. She was standing in the centre of the stage, alone except for the duke.

And then it was over. A strange, adolescent awkwardness fell over them. He cleared his throat. She straightened her skirt. They both glanced at the door and then back to each other. 'I trust I have demonstrated the need for further decoration?' he said.

She touched her lips. And against her better judgement, she nodded.

'Shall I get a bit of ribbon? I am nearly tall enough to

reach that hook without a ladder. Or I could steady you while you place it on the hook,' he offered.

She imagined how easy it would be for him to lift her, and her slow slide down his body once the job was done, leaving them standing close again, under the white berries. 'I will get you a ladder.'

Chapter Seven

She had tasted of iced cakes and ginger and smelled of woodsmoke and brandy. Montford turned the branch in his hands, staring at it. How long had it been since he had kissed a pretty girl under the mistletoe, just for the fun of it?

He had done it last Christmas, of course. His own house had mistletoe boughs in several doorways. It was pleasant for both parties to catch a young lady under the berries, to swing her briefly off her feet and buss her on the cheek.

If the girl was not willing and wandered beneath the bough in mistake, he would make a playful start for her and send her scampering in fright before she realised that it was naught but a game. Then they would both laugh. And sometimes he would get his kiss after all, if she came back to award him for his good humour.

But had any of those previous kisses been as this one? It was sweet and sad at the same time, tasting of lost youth and aged like wine on his tongue. But there was hope in it as well, reminding him that while he might never be a boy again, there was much to enjoy in the present. The clock had not precisely stopped when he'd kissed Generva Marsh. But the passage of time had not felt quite so loud and insistent.

When he had pulled away from her he'd seen the same thing mirrored in her eyes. Her needs might have changed over the years. But the desire to be loved, and to love in return, had not diminished.

He had kissed her. For a moment, the title had fallen away and he'd felt like nothing more than a man. But he was a man without a wife. And for the first time in a long time, he felt incomplete. Both of his courtships, while not devoid of romance, had been foregone conclusions. He had shown interest and they had been flattered. He had proposed and they had accepted. It had all been very simple.

But that was the past. He had consoled himself that he was too old to start again. It had been a lie. But to open his heart when the answer was not guaranteed…

There was a shifting from behind him and a whispered, 'Your Grace?'

He turned, surprised that he was not alone in the room.

It was Gwendolyn, holding a step stool in front of her. 'Mama said you needed a ladder.'

So Mrs Marsh had lost her nerve and sent the girl to deal with him. Perhaps she still hoped that there would be a match between them and that a moment alone in the presence of mistletoe would be the answer. She was wrong.

But that was no fault of Generva's. 'Of course,' he said, smiling. He took the stool from her and climbed it to hang the branch on a nail above the door. Then he stepped down again, standing well clear of the thing so that he might talk to the girl in peace. 'And while I have you alone, I wish to speak with you for a moment.' He gestured to the chairs by the window and they sat.

He resisted the urge to clear his throat, fearing that it would make him seem even more old and pompous than he already felt. 'I wanted to apologise personally for the actions of my nephew.'

He could see, in the bright afternoon light, that her eyes were still red from crying. But for the moment, at least, they remained dry.

'That is not necessary. They were not your fault after all.'

'He is my heir and it reflects poorly upon my family

that he used you, in such a way. I wish to make it right, if that is possible.'

'I fail to see how you can,' she said with a sad smile. 'The man is already married. Even if he were not, I doubt I would take him back after how he has treated me.'

'I understand that,' he said as gently as possible. 'Nor would I wish you to. It disappoints me to say so, but had I known of his courtship from the beginning, I would have warned you away from him.'

'Because you did not think me worthy?' She seemed ready to take offence.

He hurried to put her at her ease. 'On the contrary. It is he who is not worthy. I had hoped on hearing that he meant to marry that it would be otherwise. But he has proved my worst fears and toyed with your affections. I must do what I can to make reparation.'

She gave him another sad smile that made her seem older than her years. 'That is very kind of you, Your Grace. Mama said something on the subject to me already. If you mean to propose, I beg that you do not. It will save us both the embarrassment when I refuse.'

He hoped the relief he felt was not as obvious as it seemed. 'You would not accept such an offer? You would be a duchess, you know. It is what Tom would have made you on my death.'

She shuddered. 'Let us not talk of that, either. You are in good health at the moment, are you not?'

'And I hope to be so, for some time,' he said. 'All the same, you would have been the duchess eventually.'

'I hope you do not think that was an enticement when I accepted your nephew. I saw nothing further than the man in front of me.' She smiled again. 'I proved myself a very poor judge of character.'

'If gentlemen behaved as they ought, it would not be necessary for ladies to be on guard,' he reminded her. 'And it is unfair that your reputation should suffer from his cavalier treatment of you.'

She gave a slight nod to say that he was too kind.

'There will be a settlement,' he said, stopping her before she could speak. 'I will not accept a refusal of that, after the mortal blow you have dealt me by refusing my hand. You wound me to the quick, miss, for though I am old enough to be your father, I do not like to be reminded of the fact.'

She hurried to deny the fact, then noticed his smile and relaxed at the shared joke. 'Very well, Your Grace. I thank you for your concern.'

'I have another plan that might suit you better,' he said, trying not to sound as cryptic as he felt. 'I do not wish to speak of it as yet. But if I could repair your reputation in some other way, one that would give your broken heart time to heal and not trap you in a marriage not of your choosing, would you accept my help?'

Her shoulders sagged as well-disguised tension was

released from them. 'If such a thing was possible, I would accept it gladly, Your Grace.'

He rose and offered her his hand. She rose as well, and he escorted her to the door. 'Then I shall endeavour to do my best for you.' He glanced up to see the mistletoe that he had hung only a few minutes ago. 'And now, you must indulge an old man, if only for luck.' He laid a finger to direct her and she went up on tiptoe to kiss him, a brief, daughterly peck on the cheek.

He responded with a fatherly kiss on the top of her head. 'Merry Christmas, my dear. Do not worry, I will make all right.'

She all but scampered as she left him, and he reached thoughtfully up to pluck one of the berries and toss it into the fire.

Seven, eight, nine...

Generva stared suspiciously up at the mistletoe, counting the berries there. She was sure there had been ten when she had left the room earlier in the day. She held her breath as she peered around at her feet to make sure the berry had not dropped off and rolled away. There was no sign of it on the floor.

She resisted the urge to move the furniture just to make sure. It was a roundabout solution to a perfectly simple problem. If she wished to know if a kiss had occurred after the meeting between the duke and her daughter, she had but to go and ask Gwen.

Strangely, she did not want to. She had left them alone together so that the matter of the proposal could be properly settled. But she had trusted that he would behave as a gentleman, especially if the answer was no. If he had pressed his advantage, as he had when Generva had been alone with him, she could not ignore it. She would explain to her daughter that what might have been a simple Christmas game last season might now be seen as permission to take even greater liberties. If she had agreed to a marriage, then it must occur tomorrow as scheduled.

If not? Then Generva would inform the duke that he must offer again and allow no second refusal. The girl would likely pout and sulk. But in the end she would have a husband who was both rich and powerful, and good-humoured, as well. He had a friendly, almost playful nature, and an excellent singing voice. Smiles came easily to her when he was around, and she was not normally given to such frivolity.

She was waxing on his virtues again. It netted her nothing. If she must speak of them at all, it would be to Gwen. After his marriage to her daughter, she could brag of the match to the jealous mothers of less-fortunate girls.

Perhaps Gwen would not have the grand passion she hoped for. But it was well past the time for romance. If she married the duke, she would have kindness and security, and never feel the desolation of the soul that came with knowing one was alone. The women of the Marsh household, both of them, must stop behaving like silly, love-struck maidens and face facts.

'Are you looking for something?'

She jumped at the sound of his voice, placing her hand over her suddenly heaving bosom.

The duke was glancing down at the floor, just as she had as she searched for the berry. 'I am sorry to startle you. But it seemed, just now, that you were searching for something. May I be of assistance?'

Darling, it has been a long time...

A sudden image flashed into her head of John, returned from sea. He would smile and coax her to the bedroom, claiming he needed help removing his boots. She would smile and follow, and they would close the door, even if it was the middle of the afternoon....

Why, of all times, must she think of such a thing? And why, in the presence of this particular man? The answer was obvious. But she was sure, somewhere on the other side of the veil, her husband was laughing at her.

She caught her breath and swallowed. 'The room needs sweeping. It was foolish to decorate before giving it a good cleaning.' She looked up into his face, which was very near hers, and leaned back into the door frame to keep from falling.

'I shall bring the broom from the kitchen, if you promise not to strike me again.' He was smiling, as though they shared a secret joke.

Her heart was beating so loud and fast she feared he must hear it from where he stood. She braced her shoulders against the woodwork, leaning back into the solidness of the house. 'That will not be necessary. It has been a most confusing week,' she added, hoping this would explain her behaviour.

'It has indeed,' he replied. 'And I suppose you are wondering the results of my conversation with your daughter just now.'

'I…' What was the answer to this? Courtesy suggested that she deny curiosity, but her duty as a mother was just the opposite. She swallowed and attempted another breath. 'Yes, I am.'

'While she is a lovely girl, I fear our first hope was in vain. She has little interest in wedding me and I would not persuade her against her will. She is still quite young, and full of romantic illusions, as we all were at that age.'

'She will outgrow them in time,' Generva said firmly, thinking of how far her own life had veered from young romance.

'Perhaps. Or perhaps not. She deserves a chance at a love match, does she not? And a man who can prove that all of us are not such bounders as my nephew proved to be.'

'But how will that be possible? Tomorrow people will be talking of nothing else but her jilting.'

His finger was on her lips now, resting gently to silence them. 'I will make sure the blame falls where it belongs, with my erstwhile heir. And—' he gave her a smile that was both reassuring and secretive '—I have another plan in mind. Something that will occupy the gossips for weeks to come.'

'But...' If she had forgotten the finger resting against her lips, this attempt at speech made her immediately aware of it. The movement of her mouth dragged across the skin of it, and she had a sudden, totally irrational desire to touch it with her tongue, to take it into her mouth and suck.

Perhaps he had a similar thought. For though his smile did not falter, his already dark eyes seemed to grow darker. 'Do you trust me?'

She should not. She should ask him about the missing berry. But she gave the barest of nods. And again, the friction of her lips on his hand made her mind wander.

'Then you must not fear,' he said. His hand dropped away from her face to rest upon her shoulder. 'And you must not take everything upon yourself.'

'Who else has there been to help me?' she said, unable not to rail, just a little, at the unfairness of widowhood.

'No one yesterday,' he agreed. 'But today you must remember that you are no longer alone.'

She wanted to argue that of course she was still alone. John had been captain at sea, but she had always been the captain of her own little ship right here in Redding-ton. While it might seem that she deferred to him, he would soon be gone. Today or tomorrow, St Stephen's Day at the latest, he would be on his horse, riding south, and she would be alone again.

His hand tightened upon her shoulder ever so gently, the thumb settling in the hollow of her collarbone and stroking. 'You knew the old song I was singing before, did you not?'

She nodded again, barely able to breathe.

'It was a man's song. The man is the holly. The woman is the ivy, who clings to him for support.'

She did not need to, she reminded herself. But it would be pleasant, for a time, to cling to anyone.

'That song is rather unfair to poor ivy, for she is stand-ing outside the door with cold fingers. But do you know the chorus?' he asked softly.

At the moment, she was not sure she knew anything, other than that the duke had the beginning of a beard shadow, just under the curve of his full lower lip. Her eyes dropped to the ground again, so she would not have to stare at his mouth.

'"Let Holly have the mastery, as the manner is."' The words were barely a breath against her hair. 'That is what you must do for me, Generva. Let me help you.'

His thumb travelled up her shoulder until it rested under her chin, and tipped her face towards his.

She should not be doing this.

She allowed herself one token protest before putting it aside and closing the last inch between them to accept his kiss. His mouth was warm and wonderful, and the nearness of his body as comforting as a blanket on a winter night. She leaned into him and felt his hand on the small of her back, supporting her as he opened her mouth, capturing her tongue with a lazy possessiveness, drawing it back into him so that she might kiss him as he was kissing her.

He tasted of mulled wine and mischief, and she gave herself over to it, wrapping her arms around his neck so that their hips touched. She felt his body stir against her belly, growing hard. He wanted her in that way?

Her heart and mind warred for a moment, trying to decide whether to be offended or flattered. If she was not careful, she would have a reputation more damaged than her daughter's. The world would think she was one of those too-gracious widows, willing to let a man warm her bed for favours.

In the end, her body won out over reason. Her knees weakened, pressing her hips ever so slightly in welcome towards the budding erection.

'What are you doing?' Ben was sitting on the stairs in the hall, watching the whole scandalous moment.

She broke quickly from his kiss, straightening her skirts and touching her hair. Then she cursed herself for the fussiness. It made her look even more guilty than she felt.

The duke was given to no such sudden movements. He was still staring down at her, eyes pools of blackness, a slight satisfied smile upon his lips. 'I am kissing your mother,' he said to the boy, as if it was the most natural thing in the world to be caught in an embrace in the middle of the day.

'Oh,' Ben responded. Perhaps that was just the way to handle such a thing, for her son did not seem the least bit surprised. His tone said that such carrying on was not nearly as interesting as catching wrens in the woods.

'Like you kissed my sister before?'

Generva pushed away so fast that her head hit the door frame. 'Your Grace.' There was much more that she wanted to say, and none of it was appropriate for little ears. For now, two words would have to be enough to tell him what she truly thought of the sort of man that would do such a terrible thing. Then she gave him another push for good measure and fled past her son, up the stairs to her room.

Chapter Eight

Montford stood in the doorway, lips still warm and body still alert from the effects of her kiss. It had been a promising beginning. But the conclusion had been both unexpected and unfortunate. He turned to look at the boy on the stairs. 'No, actually, kissing your mother was quite different from kissing your sister.'

'Oh.' The boy seemed no more interested than he had been without the explanation. He took a pair of conkers from his pocket, tapping them together then holding one out to the duke. The smack of nut against nut punctuated the silence.

Montford sighed and walked to the stairs to sit at the boy's side, taking one of the strings. 'When I kissed your sister, it was out of kindness, as a father would have.'

'You are not her father,' Ben pointed out, taking a few tentative swings at his opponent's nut. 'Papa is dead.'

'That is true,' the duke agreed. 'You are the man of the house now.'

The sound of the nuts stopped suddenly.

'It is an awful lot of work, watching out for the two of them, is it not?' the duke suggested, swinging his conker back to tap the boy's.

There was more silence from the boy, as though he was only just realising that he might be the watcher, and not the one to be watched over. Then, slowly, he nodded. 'They do not listen to me,' he whispered.

'Even when you are right, as you were when you did not like my nephew,' the duke agreed. 'But you are still the man of the house, when all is said and done. That is why I must come to you now.'

The boy gave him a wide-eyed, blank look.

'What you just saw, when your mother and I were under the mistletoe, was not quite proper of me. You were right to stop us.'

The boy gave a confused look over his shoulder, towards the place his mother had retreated. Then he turned back and cracked his conker hard against the one the duke was holding.

'She will thank you. And she will forgive me eventually, I am sure.' At least he hoped she would. There was much more to be discussed before the matter could be settled between them. 'But for now, if we are to do this properly, you must ask my intentions.'

The boy gave him another confused look, the nut hanging still on the string before him.

The duke began again. 'When I kissed your sister, it was as a friend. It was very innocent. But she is unmarried, as am I, and some people might wonder.'

'But you are old,' the boy said, as though this explained everything.

'Not so old as all that,' the duke said, trying not to growl. Then he added, 'If you see such things in the future, and you are not sure they are proper, you have but to clear your throat and give a disapproving look. It will stop things before there is trouble.' He demonstrated and the boy shrank back in alarm.

He smiled again. 'Or you can just be a damned little nuisance. It works almost as well at breaking up liaisons, and you are very good at it.'

The boy smiled back, swinging the nut back and forth in a low arc, quite pleased with his own cleverness.

'But if you were to see something as you just saw between myself and your mother?' The duke gave a gentle smile. 'That was somewhat more serious. As such, you had a right to ask what I was doing.'

'I did that,' the boy pointed out.

'And I told you,' the duke said. 'But honour also requires me to tell you of the esteem in which I hold your mother. And to request your permission to court her.'

The boy stared at him in thoughtful silence. The conker swung back and forth like a pendulum.

For a moment, Montford wondered what he might do should the boy refuse. Clout the little beggar on the ear, perhaps. He was owed at least one good whack for the boot he'd delivered in the parlour.

'You want to court my mother,' the boy said, making a small face. 'That is well and good for you. But what does that mean to me?'

It was a legitimate question. 'I suppose, should we marry, I would be your stepfather.'

'I can manage without one,' Benjamin answered solemnly.

'Right enough.' The boy was a surprisingly hard bargainer. 'But at least, with me, you are being consulted. At some point, your mother might choose one for you and give you no say in the matter.'

'True, that,' the boy agreed.

'If you were to agree to me, I could take your troublesome sister off your hands, as well. I will find her a proper husband.' He thought for a moment. 'One that does not kick dogs.'

'At least then she would stop crying over the last one,' Ben agreed. 'What else?'

What else? He could offer a large house, a proper

education, a possible knighthood and a solid career in anything that might interest the child. But he doubted any of those would tempt. 'I have a manor in Sussex with a very nice piece of land attached to it. There are woods with trees fit for climbing.' He looked over at the boy. 'I climbed them myself, when I was your age. Also a pond, with as many frogs as you might want, and a stream for fishing.'

'I have never been fishing,' the boy admitted. 'When Papa was home, there was never time.' Was that wistfulness he heard in the child's tone?

'Your father was the captain of a ship, was he not?'

The boy nodded.

'He was a very busy man. I am but a duke and—' *other than running the country, and keeping my tenants housed and hundreds of servants fed and clothed* '—I have more than enough time to fish. In summer, when the weather is good, we will live in the country and I will teach you.'

The boy brightened.

'Do I have your blessing?' the duke prompted.

'Yes, sir.'

'You must call me Your Grace,' he reminded the boy. 'At least until we can settle on something more fitting that your mother will agree to.'

'Yes, My Grace,' the boy said with a slanted smile

meant to annoy. Then he delivered a solid whack with his conker and split the duke's nut in two.

'Hot cockles,' the duke said, and slapped him lightly on the back of the head. 'Now I must go and try to mend the damage you did to your mother's heart by making her think I loved your sister better than her. Keep your mouth shut on this for a day or two and you shall be gutting your own trout by May.'

The boy made a gesture of a key turning on his locked lips, grabbed the conkers and ran for the kitchen.

Christmas Eve dinner was less formal and more tense than the one on the previous evening. Mrs Marsh remained locked in her room, leaving Mrs Jordan to see to the children and the meal. It seemed the housekeeper had also been instructed to prevent further misbehaviour by Montford, for she was present in the dining room more than she was absent, adding and removing plates and sides as diligently as a footman.

She should, at least, have been appreciative of the meal he had provided for them. He had ordered a fully cooked goose from the village baker to make up for the roast that had been served to him the night before. She had smiled and thanked him when it had been delivered to the kitchen, along with a hamper that contained oranges, chestnuts and an iced Christmas cake.

But then Generva had announced her megrim and

the whole house had turned against him. Not the whole house, perhaps. Gwendolyn and Mrs Jordan might look on him with suspicion. But Ben still seemed to enjoy his company, as did the spaniel.

After the meal, they retired to the parlour for cards and games. Mrs Jordan stationed herself in the corner with a bag of knitting like a *tricoteuse* beneath the guillotine, enjoying his suffering.

Was it not punishment enough that Generva refused to speak with him? He had delivered apologies and explanations through her bedroom door, well aware of the scene he was creating by lingering in the upper hallway. Her only response was to whisper that he was making things worse and demand that he please go away.

He suspected she meant to hide from him until he quit the house. He had no intention of doing so. If he remained until Christmas morning, she would have to come down for church. She would not permit her children to avoid the service, nor would she send Gwendolyn alone to face the gossips. When she opened the door, he would be there for her. All things would be settled at once.

It was almost a relief when he caught Ben yawning and Mrs Jordan announced that it was time for bed. Each hour passed meant an hour closer to the moment he might see her again. But that was before he remembered that the next eight hours would be spent in cold discomfort, sharing a narrow mattress with a boy and a dog.

After an hour's tossing and turning, he rose, pulling his coat over his nightshirt, in lieu of a dressing gown.

'Where are you going?' Ben asked in a sleepy voice.

'To the sofa, in the parlour,' he replied. 'You snore and your feet smell.'

'Good riddance,' the boy said, moving to the centre of his mattress.

Montford smiled, for he had expected no less. Then he shut the door and walked down the hall to the place he most wished to be. He put his hand to the knob and paused as his confidence faltered.

Was it normal, at this point in life, to be nervous about such a thing? He had kissed women before. When the kisses were pleasant enough, and the women willing, he sometimes took them to bed. It was sport and nothing more.

But tonight would likely be different. To find a woman that he desperately wanted to kiss was a novelty. To want more than just a night's entertainment was a miracle. But never in his life had he feared rejection. He was the Duke of Montford, damn it all.

He smiled. His title amounted to nothing. There was nothing in his past to prepare him for Mrs Marsh. He did not bother to knock this time, for he did not want to make a single sound that was not necessary. Instead, he opened the door slowly, relieved that it did not squeak, and whispered into the darkness, 'Generva, may I come in?'

Chapter Nine

The case clock in the hall was striking eleven. Generva tossed in bed and stuffed her pillow into her ears, but she could not manage to escape the fact that she was one hour closer to Christmas. Tomorrow morning would be awful, for they would be forced to face the disapproving stares and whispered innuendos from the other churchgoers.

But she doubted that it could be much worse than the afternoon had been. She had been all but rubbing herself against a man in full view of her ten-year-old son. And then, to find that he had been kissing her own daughter just scant minutes before…

She had been weak. Weak and foolish. The whole house must know of it now, for he had shouted apologies through the door for nearly an hour. Well, not shouted, perhaps. But with that voice of his, even quiet declarations of his innocence had seemed embarrassingly loud. Once the door was shut, she had found the strength to refuse him that she had lacked while in the parlour. She had told him to go away.

But he had not. He'd stayed for dinner and she had stayed in her room. The aroma coming up through the floor smelled suspiciously like roast goose. Her hunger must be affecting her senses. There was nothing of the kind in the larder. Succulent flesh, crispy brown skin, stuffing with chestnuts, gravy, smooth on the tongue…

Foolishness. Why did she insist on longing for things she could not have? And why did her stomach ache so for missing just one meal? She refused to believe that she missed anything else enough to lay awake pining for it.

Then the door of her room opened. And it was him, whispering, 'Generva, may I come in?'

'Yes.'

No. The answer was supposed to be an unequivocal negative. But she'd answered with her heart and not her brain, and now she could hear the sound of garments dropping to the floor and feel the weight of a man sitting on the edge of her bed. At last, she remembered that she should be outraged. 'Your Grace, what are you doing?'

'When I first arrived, you offered me your bed. I have

decided to accept it.' She could hear the smile in his voice.

'You know this is not what I meant,' she whispered. 'I was not planning to be here with you.'

'It will be much warmer if you remain,' he announced, and ran a pair of startlingly cold feet along her bare leg.

'Stop that.' She tried to pull the sheet up and her night-gown down simultaneously, only to feel his arm slip around her shoulders.

'This is much better,' he insisted into her ear.

He was right. This was better. She shivered from head to toe, not with the cold, but the utter delight of feeling that deep voice rumbling against her temple.

It was also wrong. He could not toy with the affections of her or Gwendolyn. She would tell him so and send him from the house. And she would do it…

The arm on her shoulders slipped to the small of her back.

…in the morning. Her conscience grumbled. But common sense answered that she would have to wake the whole house if she wished to turn him out now. If he was gone after breakfast, he could do no more harm. And until then? It was Christmas. This would be her gift to herself.

She stretched against him in welcome. In response, she felt him smile. 'Now, will you allow me to explain the events of this afternoon?'

All he wished to do was talk? 'If you must,' she said, sounding as cross as she felt.

'Before I kissed you, I spoke to your daughter and we agreed a union between us would be quite impossible. When we parted, she kissed me on the cheek and I kissed her hair. It was all quite innocent. But apparently Benjamin witnessed it. Boys, being what they are, he could not wait to tattle.'

'Oh.' That was one worry removed, at least. 'Thank you,' she added. 'Now, if that is all…'

He laughed. 'You know that was not my only reason for coming here.' He rolled so that she was on top of him, and she felt the solid weight of his member settle between her thighs.

'I cannot,' she said, not wishing him to know how easy it had been to accept his seduction. Her voice was the only firmness in her, for her entire body seemed to be melting at his touch. She grew slick at the gentle nudge of his arousal, her body opening to it, eagerly awaiting that first push that would join them.

'Perhaps you will change your mind once I have told you the rest of my plan.'

He was still talking? Why would he not simply kiss her so that she might surrender?

'Next Season, your daughter will be in London. She will be the most eligible catch at Almack's because she will have my sponsorship.' His fingers were playing with the buttons of her nightdress. 'You will be there as well, to chaperone. And I have promised Ben that he shall fish in my trout stream.'

Her mind struggled to understand what he was suggesting. Did he expect her to trade her honour for his patronage? Now that they had got to this point, it was hardly necessary to bargain. She had not felt the touch of a man for a full six months before John had died. Since then, there had been no offers, only the pitying looks of other women and the encouragement from the vicar to immerse herself in good works. As though that was any protection against the need she had felt on long winter nights like this.

She did not want or need Montford's help. She was not the sort of woman who would spread her legs for a trip to London. The idea that she might sell herself so cheaply was disgusting.

But that did not change the way she felt about the act itself. To be held and cosseted and kissed, for a few hours at least, would be wonderful. It had been so long that she had lost hope it would ever happen again. How long might it be before another such offer came? And that it should come from a man so good and kind, and so thoroughly attractive…

'Let us not speak of the future. I cannot bear to think about it tonight,' she said, for it was perfectly true. 'It is late.' To encourage him, she arched her back, pushing her hips gently into him.

'Of course,' he whispered. 'We can discuss it all on the way to church tomorrow. But tonight...' He kissed her, again, and it was a question. Was he permitted to continue?

It had been good in the parlour. It was even better in bed, when she was spread over his naked body like a blanket, soaking in the heat of his skin. To answer him, she ran a cautious hand down his arm, and back up, along his side. It was different than what she was used to. He had a thicker torso with both muscle and wealth. Not youthful, but still firm. His arms were strong; she could feel the muscles bulge in them. The thighs beneath her legs were strong from riding. She widened hers and settled her legs around them.

Satisfied that she was willing, his hands swept down and up her body, stripping the nightdress away, so that there might be nothing between them. It felt so good, she wanted to scream with pleasure, and they had not even begun. 'We must be careful,' she whispered. 'I would not want to do anything that might wake the household.'

'I would be...very...very...quiet.' A trail of kisses punctuated his words. They travelled down her chin, to the hollow of her throat, and lower. He slipped his hands beneath her arms and slid her body higher so that he could nuzzle her breasts. His lips closed on a nipple and sucked gently.

She had forgotten how good it was. The tightening in her breasts. The readying of the muscles deep inside her. In the dark, she could imagine the smile on his face as he kissed her, and the fire in her heart, banked low for so long, was blazing again. It took only a moment, and a single touch of his thumb between her legs, and she was spiralling into a short, sweet climax.

Against her breast, she felt him laugh.

He must think her the most simple kind of trollop to succumb so quickly. 'I am not the sort of woman who...' she began.

'I rather think that you might be,' he said, licking the underside of her breast. And then his hands travelled down again, stroking more persistently, spreading her, fingertips dipping inside.

She was losing control and was quite unwilling to tell him to stop. At least not until he had finished what he was doing and that sweet bubble of pleasure burst in her again. She clamped her thighs against his hand and pushed, giving herself over to it, taking selfishly from him.

He gave her a moment's peace then, to collect her thoughts. 'Do you still wish me to leave?' he asked. 'For it would be most inhospitable of you.'

She wanted to argue that hospitality did not normally

extend to spreading one's legs for any man that happened by the kitchen door. But he was not just any man. She slid back down his body so that she could touch him, learning his secrets. She stroked and caressed, tracing veins, circling him with her fingers and teasing until she was sure he must be near to bursting. Then she took him deep within her body.

For a moment they stayed completely still, in mutual amazement, and then they began to move. Slowly at first, then eagerly, then with desperate, violent speed. He pulled her face down to his so that they might smother their groans of pleasure in a kiss. They loved in silence, except for the soft creaking of the ropes beneath the mattress.

Suddenly, his back arched and he released inside her. There had been no attempt to withdraw, nor had she wished him to. But the intimacy of the act brought her the third orgasm of the evening.

When she was sure he had finished, she rolled off him to lie on her back, at his side. From the hall, the clock struck twelve.

His face turned to nip her ear. 'Thank you, Generva, for the best Christmas gift I've got in years.'

'You're welcome, Your Grace,' she said, still trying catch her breath.

He snorted softly. 'Under the circumstances, I think you have earned the right to call me Thomas.'

'Of course, Your Grace,' she said. It was a shame it was too dark for him to see her smile.

He chuckled again. 'It's to be that way, is it?' His finger traced the length of her arm before inching towards her breast, drawing an ever-narrowing circle in search of her nipple. 'Are we to play the randy peer and the proper housewife? I have no objection to it, if it is easier for you.' His fingers closed in a pinch that made her back arch. Then he rolled to face her, trapping her body beneath him. 'There is no escape for you now, Mrs Marsh. Spread your legs so that I may have my wicked way with you again.'

Chapter Ten

It was still dark when he left her bedroom, rolling to kiss her lips before swinging his legs to the floor to search for his nightshirt.

Without thinking, she held her arms out to him.

In the dim light of the fire, she saw him shake his head. 'I must be gone before the servants are up. I promised no gossip, remember?'

'And where shall you go?'

'To the sofa in the parlour. I will pull a rug over myself and sleep there.' He grinned at her. 'It will shock Mrs Jordan when she comes to lay the fire. But there are worse shocks, are there not?'

But would she be so shocked, really? The poor woman must have guessed the reason for Generva's sudden indisposition yesterday. What would she think if the duke announced his plan to take them all to London for the Season?

She should not have silenced him when he had begun to speak of it. She should have refused immediately, so they might have enjoyed each other with no misunderstanding between them. In the cold light of morning, the memory of his suggestion made something special seem like a different, more elegant sort of disgrace.

He was standing over the bed, staring down at her as she brooded. 'Might I trouble you for a last kiss before I go?'

He bent down, and she gave him an embarrassed peck upon the cheek. 'Goodnight, Your Gr— Thomas.'

If he was disappointed by the lack of warmth, it did not show. 'Good morning, Generva,' he corrected. 'And a very good one, I hope.' With that, he was gone.

She began to miss him the moment the door closed. The night had been a mistake, one that she should have stopped immediately. What sort of an example was she to either of her children that she would bed a man she had known for less than two days? And how would she go on without him once he was gone?

But the senior Thomas Kanner was the sort of man that made one forget all that. It had been good to lie with a man again. But it had been amazing to lie with this particular man. When the sun rose, she would find herself humming the old carols he was so fond of, with their faintly sad melodies and their fearless welcoming of the darkness that came with the brightness of this season. When she looked in the mirror as she washed, she would smile. She might not be in the spring of her life, but neither had she reached winter. She was alive and happy to be so.

When she saw him again at the breakfast table, he was as jolly as ever. He greeted both children warmly and even coaxed a smile from Gwendolyn. But he gave no indication that anything had changed between them, other than a certain tenderness in his eyes as he looked at her.

But the song he had been singing as he shaved was about a maid in a lily-white smock opening the door to him. For Christmas morning, it was most improper. She hoped that he did not mean to sing when they were at church. Perhaps he could be persuaded to do some plainsong or chant that Reverend Allcot might not find so reactionary.

Then she recalled that she had not asked him his plans. 'Will you be accompanying us to church, Your Grace?'

'Of course,' he replied with a smile. 'I will be there for the wedding.'

Gwendolyn's fork clattered to her plate, and she reached for a napkin as though ready to stifle a sob.

'There is to be no wedding,' Generva hissed. 'I thought it was settled.'

'Not for your daughter, perhaps.' He looked at her with mock surprise. 'But I thought you and I had reached an agreement on the subject last night.'

'You and I. We. Today.' Was that what he had meant when talking of a trip to London and a Season for Gwen? Their discussion had been sorely lacking in detail.

'I am sorry if we are causing you pain by taking the day that was to have been yours,' he said to her daughter in the gentlest of voices. 'But there is no better way to deflate a scandal than by creating a bigger one. As the stepdaughter of a duke, I suspect you shall have your pick of gentlemen when you are ready to choose one.'

'You and Mama are getting married?' Gwen seemed surprised, but not unhappy. 'How wonderful. I do not mind. Not at all, Your Grace.'

'I gave my permission,' Ben said around a mouthful of bacon. 'Because I am man of the house.'

Generva was choking on her piece of toast. Even after she had managed to wash the bite down with a sip of tea, she could not seem to get air into her lungs. Her future had been settled to the satisfaction of everyone in the house. Even Mrs Jordan had heard the news and come in from the kitchen to congratulate His Grace on a wonderful plan.

It was a fairy tale after all, and she was the princess

in need of rescue. Or perhaps she was a duchess, since he was not a prince.

And that was nonsense. All of it. There was no magic in the world. Wishes were not granted and miracles did not happen, even at Christmas. She could not even call it an answered prayer, since she had long ago given up praying that a man would come to change her name and her life.

Once again, common sense answered. But this time, it was with a laugh. Generva could not very well refuse him. It was too late for that. Nor could she announce that they had settled no such thing, last night.

One could not be forced, in the heat of passion, to make such a momentous decision.

Or perhaps one could.

But when one was a chaste widow, not supposed to be feeling the heat of passion at all...?

Then perhaps one must be sensible and keep one's mouth firmly shut.

They finished their breakfast and pulled on bonnets and coats for the mile-long walk to church. At the first opportunity, Generva pulled Mrs Jordan aside and begged her to walk a short distance behind with the children so that she might speak privately with the duke.

The woman gave a smile and a knowing nod, completely misinterpreting their need for privacy.

Thomas misunderstood her as well, folding her arm

into the crook of his elbow as though walking arm in arm with her was the most natural thing in the world.

When she was sure they were far enough ahead so that they might not be overheard, she whispered, 'Are you mad?'

'No more so than the next man,' he replied. 'Do you fear for the sanity of our children? Because we will need to have a son, if you do not wish to see more of young Tom Kanner.'

'Children.' She had been a fool not to think of that last night when they were being so careless in their love-making.

'You do like children, do you not? You have two, of course. You seem to enjoy them well enough. It is a great comfort to me that you survived both the births and the upbringing. I suspect you are made of sterner stuff than the two duchesses who precede you.'

'Duchesses,' she said. That was what she would be, should they marry. Not a fairy-tale princess, but the very real Duchess of Montford.

'Think of the advantages to Gwendolyn and Benjamin.' He was speaking quickly, as though he feared that he must plead and win the case before they arrived at the church door.

'I cannot,' she said. 'We cannot.' It was as it had been at breakfast; she could not breathe. They were still travelling forward, down the road to the church. But she felt like a leaf on the tide, being dragged along against her will.

'Are you not at least fond of me?' He seemed taken aback by the thought. 'I am sure you will find me the most amiable of husbands.' Then he smiled.

'It is not that,' she said hurriedly, trying to ignore the little rush she felt when he smiled at her. 'It is just that…' And what was it, precisely? 'It is so sudden,' she said at last.

'Not really,' he answered. 'I am near to fifty. To have waited half a century to feel the way I do is a long wait indeed.'

He felt something for her. Apparently, it was more than friendship and more than lust. 'You have been married before,' she reminded him.

'Each time, it was different. And this…' He gave a helpless shrug of his shoulders. 'What I feel for you is different. It is sudden, as you say. But it is strong. And I have never been so sure of a thing in my life as I am when I look at you. Life is fleeting. Why should we wait?'

Why indeed? She knew what he spoke of, for she felt it, as well. Since the day he had walked into her kitchen, she had been caught in the sort of giddy, headlong rush she had not felt since she was a girl. But was it wise to trust such feelings?

He sensed her doubt and patted the hand that rested on his elbow. 'Marry me. It will be fine. You shall see.'

'So you keep saying,' she replied. 'But perhaps it would have been better had you told me of your intentions last night.'

'I thought I made them clear enough.' Now his smile was positively wicked. 'With my body I did thee worship. In comparison, it is but an afterthought to endow you with my worldly goods.'

Very well. They had been married in body and spirit by the time the clock had struck twelve. And she had no intention of admitting, in a churchyard, on Christmas, that she had been willing to surrender to his charms without the benefit of matrimony. 'I do not need a man to help me, Thomas Kanner,' she said, a little too primly. 'Until recently, we have done quite well on our own.' And what a lie that was. 'For you to swoop in and rescue me is entirely unnecessary.' *But most welcome.*

He gave her a look that sent the blood singing in her veins. 'Is that what I am doing? I had no idea. I was attempting to seduce you.'

'Shh,' she said, looking around her to be sure none of the villagers gathering on the path ahead of them had heard. And then she whispered, 'You succeeded.'

'That is good,' he said. 'Because once you realise how much work comes with the title, you will wonder if you have gone from the frying pan into the fire.'

'Work?' It had never occurred to her that there would be more than the title.

'The management of several houses, scores of servants, entertainments to arrange, charities to organise...' He ticked off the duties on his fingers. 'Your poor daughter would have had no idea how to go on, and you'd have ended up doing the work anyway.' He glanced down at her, a sly sidelong glance. 'And I'd have been your son-in-law. For the sake of the girl's honour, I'd have been willing to try. But it was scant hours in your presence before I realised how awkward that would have been.'

'Awkward?'

'To have such carnal thoughts about a woman who should be respected as a mother?' He shuddered.

She gave another hurried 'Hush,' and then followed with 'Good morning, Reverend Allcot! And a Merry Christmas to you.' They had arrived at the church door, and the vicar was there to greet them, eyeing the man who escorted her with obvious disapproval.

Before he could speak, Thomas supplied his own introduction. 'Allcot, is it? Good morning, Vicar. I am Montford. Let us go into the vestry. I wish to speak to you about performing a marriage.'

'But the service is about to begin.'

'Do not worry. It cannot begin without you. Nor me, for that matter.' Thomas cast a dazzling smile at the most sombre spinster in the village. 'It is not every day a duke comes to hear you preach the homily.'

If he meant to create gossip, he was succeeding. There was an audible gasp from the woman, and a whisper rippling through the parishioners lined up behind them.

And now Mr Allcot was being swept along on the same tide that carried her, until they reached the vestry and Thomas produced the licence from his pocket.

'There has been a slight change of plans, as you well know. My nephew was totally unfit to offer for young Miss Marsh.' He smiled again. 'I have no such encumbrance, nor does Mrs Marsh. So if you would do us the service of a sacrament, in the time allotted...'

Allcot glanced down at the paper before him. 'This cannot be proper. The names are wrong. Perhaps if you could reapply...'

Generva had not realised how much she had come to want the marriage until it appeared it might be impossible. The sudden sense that her heart was crashing towards the ground was proof enough of her true feelings. She inserted herself into the conversation. 'The groom's name is right, is it not, my darling Montford? Thomas Kanner was named to honour you.' She looked up at him in adoration.

He smiled back at her, reading the message in her eyes. 'That is very true. We will add my title to the line.'

He picked up a pen from the writing desk, and did so. 'There. Right as rain.'

'But the bride...' Allcot laid a bony finger beside Gwendolyn's name.

Now Thomas took up the aspergillum resting on the table and obliterated the bride with a sprinkling of holy water. 'Oh, dear. I seem to have smudged it. But we can fix it yet.'

He scrawled *Generva* in the place from which *Gwendolyn* was rapidly disappearing. 'There.' He smiled in satisfaction. 'All better.'

The vicar stared in alarm at the mangled paper. 'That cannot be proper,' he insisted in a weak voice.

'I fail to see why not,' Thomas said, all innocence. 'The licence is right. But the names were written wrong. They are correct now. For myself, I can hardly wait to upbraid Chuckles for his mistake. Over dinner, perhaps.' He turned to Generva, as if in an aside. 'You will love the man, my darling. We must entertain him as soon as we are back in London.'

'Chuckles?' she said.

'An old nickname for my friend Charles. Manners-Sutton,' he added for the benefit of the vicar.

'The archbishop?' The vicar turned as white as his alb.

'His Grace, Canterbury,' Thomas added, tapping the signature, Cantaur:, at the bottom of the paper. 'He would marry us himself, in my drawing room, if I asked.

But I do not want to wait until we have removed to London. It would be a shame to take Generva away from her home parish when there are so many who want to wish her well.'

She was not so sure of that herself. The ladies of the congregation looked more like a pack of jackals drooling for her marrow than friends eager to celebrate her good fortune.

The vicar still looked doubtfully at the marred paper. 'If you are sure that the Archbishop made a mistake...'

As if in afterthought, the duke reached into his pocket and pulled out a heavy purse, setting it on the table, then pushed it to the side as though he had already forgotten its presence. 'I am, Reverend Allcot. I am.'

As they sat later, snug in the box pew that her family shared, Generva could not imagine a better Christmas gift. Their toes were kept warm by the little stove upon the floor in front of them, but it was the feeling of a man's hand holding hers that truly warmed her heart.

Although she had dreaded the day for a week, now that it was here, she saw no censure directed towards her daughter. The recently jilted Gwendolyn sat on her other side, completely ignored and dozing through Reverend Allcot's sermon. Beside her, Ben toyed with a penknife Thomas had given him as a Christmas gift, opening and closing it, staring thoughtfully at the mahogany of the pew.

Thomas followed the boy's gaze, then reached into his pocket and produced a bar of soap. He handed it over and they all ignored the pile of shavings building up at their feet as Ben began work on an effigy of Boney, the spaniel.

Generva marvelled at his sangfroid. She suspected he was as calm and collected in Parliament as in the parlour, equally untroubled by small boys and large men. His mere presence held the entire congregation in rapt attention. But he paid no attention. He cared for no one but her. And when she looked at him, she felt the same.

At the end of the service, the congregation sat in pious silence to witness the marriage of Mrs Generva Marsh to the Duke of Montford. There was an awkward pause when Mr Allcot asked, 'Who giveth this woman?'

She was about to answer that it should hardly be necessary to be given away at this stage in her life when her son came bounding up the aisle, complete with penknife. He left a trail of soap shavings behind him like so many rose petals dropped in the aisle. 'I do.' He turned and glared back at the congregation. 'Because I am the man of the house.'

'For the moment,' Thomas added quietly. But he smiled as he said it. And when the time came for a ring, he removed an enormous ruby from his own hand and slipped it on to her finger.

When, at last, the vicar pronounced them man and wife, Generva breathed a sigh of relief. There would be no more looking back. Now that she had grown accustomed to the idea, a life with the man beside her was all that she could have wanted.

And they could begin that future whenever Mr Allcot came to the end of the ceremony. She did not remember her last wedding being quite so sombre. That had been a hurried affair, in a chapel by the London docks that many sailors claimed as their home parish.

Perhaps Mr Allcot meant to impress the visiting peer. Or was he attempting to make up for the lack of formal licence with extra prayers? He said not one psalm, but two. He delivered the blessing that they might be 'fruitful in procreation' with a look that discouraged any joy in the attempts at breeding.

And then he began to quote, at length, from Saint Paul.

It was not necessary. With three previous marriages between them, she and Thomas were well aware of their duties to each other. They were certainly better schooled than Mr Allcot, who was as yet unmarried. As the ceremony dragged on, she could feel Ben shifting from foot to foot as his patience wore thin. There was no telling what might happen when he could no longer contain himself.

Her son was not the only male bored to mischief by Mr Allcot. Next to her, Thomas still wore a benign smile. But his foot had begun to tap. It did not seem to be a sign of impatience. There was a rhythm to it, as though he kept time to a song.

Oh, dear.

As Mr Allcot exhorted her to obedience and submission for what seemed like the hundredth time, Thomas began to hum.

There were murmurs of disapproval from the congregation, but the vicar pretended not to notice, although it was clear he did. A warning to reverence her husband was delivered in a louder voice and at a faster pace, as though he meant to race the groom to the end of the service.

It was a race he was destined to lose. As he extolled the merits of a meek and quiet spirit over ornaments of gold, Thomas burst into song.

'In a manger laid, and wrapped I was
So very poor, this was my chance
Between an ox and a silly poor ass
To call my true love to my dance.'

At the mention of the silly ass, Ben burst into laughter and Mr Allcot dropped his prayer book.

And then, to prove that she had been listening to the vicar's sermon, Generva demonstrated that she was willing to follow her new husband, no matter where he might lead. She joined him on the chorus in perfect harmony.

'Sing, oh! my love, oh! my love, my love, my love,
This have I done for my true love.'

* * * * *

RUSSIAN WINTER NIGHTS

Linda Skye

Linda Skye is a travel addict and a self-proclaimed food critic with an insatiable appetite for the written word. She first developed her love for reading and writing by browsing her grandfather's dictionaries and etymology books—a habit she has yet to abandon!

Born to Filipino parents in the United States and raised in Canada, Linda is a modern-day nomad, moving across country and ocean with her military husband. She currently lives in the United Kingdom and spends her free time writing, practising digital photography, updating her food blog and dreaming of adventures at home and abroad. She has travelled throughout North America, Europe, Asia and Africa.

Linda holds a master's of education and specialises in teaching languages and literature. She has been teaching English as a Second Language, English literature and literacy courses since 2001. Though she is currently teaching part-time at a local technical college, Linda is a full-time daydreamer with a passion for the strange, mysterious and exotic.

Chapter One

Ekaterina Romanova, the eldest, most beautiful daughter of Baron Dimitri, and the niece of the reigning Empress of Russia, was standing amongst the clucking chickens outside the palace kitchens, dressed in a plain peasant smock and woollen overcoat. Her thick dark curls were unbound and tumbled carelessly down her back. Her smooth complexion was free of fashionable white powder.

If her ageing father could see her in her current unadorned state, as she stood in a place reserved for the common folk, he would probably die of a heart attack. Her mother would swoon. Her younger sisters would tut their disapproval and hide their faces in shame.

But Ekaterina simply could not care less about what they all might think of her.

'Come, children,' she called in her sweet, chime-like voice. 'Come have some bread!'

A flock of hungry children surrounded the young noblewoman, their grubby hands reaching out and their sweet, high voices calling out excitedly. For Ekaterina was passing out large steaming loaves of freshly baked bread for the children to take home to their nearly starving families.

'Bread! Bread!' the children cried, and whistled excitedly.

'Yes!' Ekaterina laughed. 'Bread! But don't push—there's enough for everyone!'

Within just a few minutes Ekaterina had nothing left in her wicker basket but crumbs. She smiled, satisfied, as thick wet snowflakes drifted down around her.

It was nearly Christmas, and the bread she had just distributed would be a boon to the families of the palace servants. She could imagine them smiling around their bland pots of stew with hot slices of crusty bread to warm their bellies, when normally they would be carefully rationing out tiny portions of grain in a desperate bid to save up enough food for the endless winter, when frost would make life nearly unbearable for most.

Hardly a happy Christmas, she mused silently.

Ekaterina resisted the urge to frown. In the North,

her father tried to treat his serfs fairly, and because of the example she saw in his policies she had always campaigned for the rights of the peasants, who were the working backbone of their livelihood. But here, at Catherine Palace, the lavish rococo residence of Russian emperors and empresses, the peasant servants were treated little better than donkeys and dogs. They were reduced to scrounging the most minimal of sustenance, accepting the crumbs that the Empress tossed their way because—simply put—there was no other choice available to them.

Ekaterina grimaced at the thought of her aunt, Empress Anna of Russia. She was a gargantuan woman, her pudgy features swollen from years of consuming the very tastiest and fattiest of foods. Ekaterina was surprised that her aunt could still breathe in her tightly laced corset.

But what was even worse than her careless, decadent lifestyle was Empress Anna's cruel and vindictive nature.

Ekaterina slowly wandered towards the edge of the walled courtyard, her delicate brows gently creasing in thought. The summons for Ekaterina to join the imperial court in the city of Tsarskoye Selo had come as an unpleasant surprise to the Romanov family in the North. Empress Anna had always distanced herself from the old nobility—especially her siblings—so her asking for her brother's eldest daughter to join the court did not bode well.

Contrary to what others might have thought, such a summons was not an honour—it was more likely a subtle declaration of war. Ekaterina, as a young, unmarried noblewoman, could be used as a political hostage—or humiliated for sport. Just last year a member of the old gentry had displeased Empress Anna in some trivial way and she had forced the elderly man to entertain her court by stripping naked and squawking like a bird in a specially constructed gilded cage. Even worse, the nobleman's extended family had abruptly and inexplicably disappeared during the harsh winter—no doubt thanks to the actions of Empress Anna's personal police squad.

Since arriving a mere week ago Ekaterina had managed to avoid close contact with her aunt, opting to stay hidden behind the jewelled plumes of the headdresses of more ambitious court women. But being inconspicuous in such a gaudy, debauched court took quite a bit of effort, and Ekaterina had not been able to help but resort to old tricks to keep her sanity—such as strolling anonymously through the peasant areas.

As she reached the edge of the walled courtyard, she heard soft, tinkling laughter. Pausing, she looked over to where a small gaggle of children were weaving pine boughs together to make crude Christmas ornaments. They were nothing like the expensive, gaudy contraptions that her aunt had commissioned for the Christmas season. Unlike those crystal baubles and bright candles, these simple decorations were dotted with crimson holly berries and strung together with tatty bits of string.

But they were even more beautiful in Ekaterina's eyes.

The children's ruddy faces shot up as she approached, her boots crunching over the freshly fallen snow. Ekaterina smiled warmly, her dainty fingertips skimming over the fragrant pine needles.

'They're beautiful, children,' she said encouragingly.

The children's smiles widened. Ekaterina patted each child on the head and leaned down to whisper.

'Come see me in the kitchens tomorrow,' she told them with a wink. 'I'll have some sweet treats for you to share.'

With that, she rose and resumed her stroll, warmed by the squeals of excited giggling in her wake. She followed the stone wall to an iron gate, which she pushed open. As she stepped through the archway, a lovely winter landscape met her eyes. Brilliantly white snow carpeted the expansive meadows, broken only by a few clusters of evergreen trees. Ekaterina stepped farther away from the palace and closer to the wilderness, relishing the cold, crisp air on her face and the bright blue sky stretching as far as the eye could see.

And then she saw him.

A man was standing in the centre of the field, his the

only tracks in the glittering snow. He was facing away from her, his thumbs hooked in his trouser pockets. Even though a cold wind stirred the fabric of his loose white shirt, he did not move—he didn't even shiver! He was so still that the white puffs of his breath were the only indication that he was a living, breathing man and not a statue.

But what a statue he would have made! His figure might have made any of those marble mythical gods envious.

Even from behind he cut a striking silhouette against the perfect blue of the horizon. He was tall, long and lean—a fact accentuated by his billowing linen shirt and fitted wool trousers. His shoulders were broad, and he had dark, tousled hair that did not quite conceal a square jaw covered in rough stubble.

Ekaterina swallowed breathlessly as he shifted his weight. And then he began to walk away, his shoes crunching over the new snow as he wandered towards the copse of trees that hid a small brook from sight.

He was leaving!

Ekaterina's feet were rooted to the spot, even though she desperately didn't want to lose sight of the stranger. She was intensely curious, but at the same time trailing after a stranger seemed a terribly dangerous idea. Ekaterina bit her lip, her brow furrowing as the distance between them grew. Should she risk revealing herself, risk her safety, for a glimpse of this handsome stranger?

Just then the man paused and turned slightly to the side. A breeze lifted his dark locks, which played across his perfect profile. Ekaterina's stomach erupted in fluttering.

Yes, she told herself. She just couldn't help herself.

Resolute and determined, Ekaterina followed him, carefully putting her feet in his large footprints so as to remain a silent and unseen follower. Although, she thought with a wry smile, he would see her immediately if he but turned around. Just a quick glimpse of his face, she told herself. A quick glance and her curiosity would be satisfied.

As she trailed after his loping strides, she found herself wondering if he would be angry at her intrusion or interested in her audacity?

Her thoughts suddenly ceased as the mystery man reached the creek, which had almost completely frozen over. She halted, expecting him to turn around and spot her, but a quacking pair of geese distracted them both. Ekaterina eyed the waddling birds quizzically. Had they neglected to migrate? How had they survived?

And then the man dug into his trouser pockets and pulled out a few crusts of bread. Clucking at the geese, he tossed the bread to the snow-covered ground and watched as the geese noisily snapped up the bits of food.

Anger awoke in Ekaterina's belly, rising like a flame to her throat. The squawking of the fat birds only increased her ire as she watched him toss another handful of crusts.

How dare he? she thought as she strode heedlessly forward. *How dare he squander such food on mere geese?*

Startled at the sound of shoes on snow, the stranger stilled and turned, his brows lifted in surprise.

'You!' Ekaterina snapped, her blue eyes fiery as she advanced on him. 'What do you think you are doing?'

The stranger held up his hands, the last few bread-crumbs falling to the ground.

'Feeding the birds,' he answered, his eyes wide.

'Feeding the birds?' Ekaterina exclaimed incredulously. 'You're feeding the birds fresh bread while the peasants are near starvation?'

The man blinked, his expression unreservedly abashed. This woman had interrupted his daily ritual of wandering out into the wilderness to feed his geese. Hearing a human voice in the cold, abandoned outdoors was unexpected…though not completely unwanted. Her voice was sweet, even in anger, and it was a welcome contrast to the harshness he'd just left behind. He'd wandered out into the countryside to escape the sweat, dust and shouting, and the cold, fresh air and natural beauty usually invigorated him. But now...he only had eyes for the firecracker burning him with her stare.

The woman before him was petite, her slight form dwarfed in her overly large wool overcoat. Her bright blue eyes were unparalleled jewels that burned with passion. His artist's eye immediately traced the pale contours of her exquisite face, from the elegant arch of her thin eyebrows to the perfect bow of her dainty lips. With midnight-black hair and a radiant complexion, she stood out in stark relief against the barren land around them. He hadn't seen her before at court—he was sure he would have noticed her if she had ever made an appearance.

Despite her slim frame and petite figure, she was a burning bundle of seething rage. He took a step back. But the woman pressed forward and reached up to jab a finger into his shoulder.

'Well?' she questioned, her voice like a sharp whip.

She reached out to poke him again, but he caught her hand in an easy grip.

'Young lady,' he began, his voice a slow, smooth velvet tone, 'I don't know who you are, but I don't see how it is any business of yours what I do with my bread. For your information, these are *my* geese. I found them with broken wings and now I have to feed them.'

Colour bloomed beautifully on her porcelain cheeks, and her ocean-blue eyes widened. Her pink lips parted in surprise and she quickly snatched her hand back, cradling it against her chest as if she had been burned. The man watched this transformation with ever-increasing interest, his desire to sketch her expressive face matched only by the primal urge to mould his hands to her hips and pull her close.

For her part, Ekaterina felt the anger drain from her body. His touch had been like fire, setting her nerves alight with an inexplicable longing. Awareness washed over her in a tingling wave as she took in the rugged slant of his thick brows, the intensity in his green eyes, the curve of his sensual lips and the hard line of his jaw.

Not a statue of a Greek god, she thought to herself, *but a living, breathing Adonis!*

He raised an inquisitive eyebrow and reality slammed back into her with the force of a tidal wave. He was a stranger in her aunt's palace and could be anyone…and *anyone* could bring malicious whispers to her aunt's itching ears.

Her face closed as her guard went up. The man's other brow lifted, his expression mildly surprised at the sudden change.

'I mean you no harm,' he said in the same steady tone. 'I am merely an employee here at the palace.'

'You work in the palace?' she asked, her facial features softening slightly.

'Yes,' he said and nodded. 'My name is Andrey.'

* * *

She studied his face, distrust in her eyes.

Andrey met her glare with an open expression, suddenly afraid that the beautiful creature before him would take flight and leave him alone in the cold. She was so refreshingly different from the women he'd met in the palace.

'Where do you work?' she asked, suspicion tingeing her tone.

'In the workshop,' he replied.

It was only a slight lie, he told himself. There was no need to expound upon the unnecessarily complicated nature of his true employment at the palace. He simply did not want to lose the chance to spend more time with her.

'The workshop?' Ekaterina almost sighed in relief.

No one in the workshop would ever brush shoulders with the nobles. It was far too dusty and dingy for the likes of Russian aristocracy. She shook off the lingering feelings of dread, banishing all thoughts of her horrible aunt. Instead, she looked upon Andrey with clear eyes. As her gaze dropped to his hands, she imagined them at work. He had long, tapered fingers and callused palms. His sleeves were rolled up to the elbow, and she could see the muscles in his taut forearms. She visualised the careful attention he would give to carving, the bulge of his upper arms as he worked the machinery and the sweat glistening on his perfect brow.

Ekaterina felt a tingle in her thighs that spread like fire through her lower belly. It ached deliciously. It twisted her stomach in knots. It made her shift from foot to foot.

'Now, if you have finished with your interrogation,' Andrey said, cutting into her thoughts in a wry tone, 'who might you be?'

Ekaterina started, looking up. Her cheeks warmed as she felt the full force of his lusty gaze. He was watching her knowingly, his intense eyes hooded. She took a moment to savour the sight of him. She would have loved to bask in the heat of his gaze but she knew it was dangerous—*oh, so dangerous*—to dally for too long.

So, lifting her chin defiantly, she turned on her heel and cast one last look over her shoulder.

'No one of interest,' she quipped.

She made as if to walk away briskly, but was stopped by a hand on her shoulder. She turned to level the stranger with a half-hearted glare, only to be met with his smouldering eyes. She swallowed, suddenly feeling light at the feeling of his fingers.

'You don't know what I'm interested in,' Andrey returned, his voice even. 'Maybe I want to have a chat with a mysterious woman in the middle of nowhere.'

Ekaterina pulled out of his grip and spun round, a frown turning down her pink lips. She inclined her head slightly, studying his chiselled face. Her mind screamed at her to leave, to turn and escape back into the palace before it was too late. But her heart and body tugged in the opposite direction; she longed to run her fingers through that thick hair, to feel the sweep of his stubbled jaw under her smooth palms, to push away his shirt and explore the mysterious expanse of muscle hidden beneath.

He was just too gorgeous.

Surely a few more minutes couldn't hurt, she told herself. After all, he was a lowly peasant and she was a hidden princess. They would probably never meet again, and no one would be the wiser about this strange encounter.

Andrey could plainly see the war in her eyes; she wanted to stay and yet felt she had to go.

I don't want her to go.

The yearning was an insistent tug, pounding like the blood in his veins. He wanted to hear her voice, feel the curve of her body against his and paint the canvas of her flesh with his lips. But she looked ready to flee, and he did not want to lose his chance. Her sweet face and honest sincerity were a balm to his frazzled nerves. He hated palace life. When it wasn't stuffy and pretentious, it was dirty and dusty. Even worse were the palace girls: their faces false with makeup and their voices forcibly high-pitched. So while the wilderness was his usual escape, he longed to spend even a few more moments with this woman.

And so, before she could make up her mind, he took her by the arms and pulled her into his chest.

Ekaterina's senses were suddenly overcome by the feeling of Andrey's hard chest against hers and the musky scent beneath his chin. She inhaled sharply, but couldn't find the resolve to pull away immediately.

'Don't go,' Andrey murmured softly.

She could barely hear him over the wild pounding of her heart. She craned her head back to look up at him and was instantly arrested by his sultry gaze. He had her pinned in place with his arms around her slim shoulders and his green eyes locked with hers. He could feel her heart beat against his chest; it was like the mad fluttering of a butterfly's wings. One of his arms slipped down to wind about her slim waist while his fingers trailed along her cheek. His fingertips were hot against her cool skin, and Ekaterina instinctively leaned into his warmth.

There was something between them: a magnetism that drew them closer and set their skin aflame with hunger. Neither could explain it, but it was warm and pulsing and perfect—as real as their breathing, which caused miniature clouds to fan across their cheeks in moist puffs of warm air. Every sense was heightened, and the hyper-awareness was a pleasurable pain.

Ekaterina shivered suddenly, and Andrey pulled her closer. He was so tall, she thought breathlessly, and his hands felt unusually large on her hips. Her knees went weak as he drew her closer, leaning in slowly as if pulled forward by an invisible force. He gathered her tightly in his strong arms, his muscles bunching under his linen shirt. He held her gaze until their noses were nearly touching…and then his lips were on hers, searching gently.

Her eyes drifted closed as the sensation of his warm mouth on hers overwhelmed her completely.

Andrey kissed her slowly, tenderly moving his lips over hers. Then he grew bolder, suckling at her bottom lip and sweeping his tongue past her lips. She obliged with innocent fervour, a small moan escaping her as he explored her mouth with his tongue. His fingers fisted in the material of her overcoat and he dragged her closer still, driven by the instinct to crush her body to his, to feel every inch of her body against his.

Not enough, his blood sang as his kisses grew in intensity.

With an impatient grunt, Andrey grabbed at the ends of her coat and pulled it open, his palms searching within the rough material. His hands met the thin cotton of a light shift and he paused. He pulled away from their fevered kiss to glance down at what he had just unveiled.

The sight made the slow rolling of desire in his stomach pitch into a full boil, spiking down his legs and up his chest. He briefly wondered why she was allowing such familiarity, but he was not about to lose his advantage. He pressed forward.

Ekaterina stood stunned in his arms, her blue eyes wide and glazed over in passion and her lips swollen and pouting from their kiss. Her long creamy neck led to a delicate collarbone. And her cotton dress swept over the rest of her body in a slightly see-through column of fabric. Had the girl no sense whatsoever? The coat had hidden her well, he mused, but the dress revealed almost all.

His impassioned eyes took in the pert swell of her unbound breasts, and the dark peaks of her stiff nipples were beads that stood out in sharp relief beneath the thin material. He could just make out the silhouette of her hourglass figure: the arc of her waist, the rise of her bottom and the sweet curves of her impossibly long legs.

He grew as hard as rock, straining uncomfortably against the scratchy material of his trousers. In awe at her beauty, he traced his fingers in invisible paint strokes over her body.

She shuddered, and he snapped.

He was on fire, and she was his only salve.

In two long strides he walked her back to the trunk of a tree, his hands cupping the backs of her thighs and his mouth ravaging hers. Her breathing hitched as he nipped at her lips with his teeth, and she twisted her fingers in his hair. He pushed his hands down her body and she twined her slim wrists at the nape of his neck. His fingers grabbed at the hem of her dress and he slid his palms up her bare legs with a groan.

He pulled at her thighs and lifted her off the ground, hooking her knees over his hips and pushing her back into the tree trunk. She arched backwards, a gasp of delight on her lips as he ground his groin into hers. He pushed her dress even higher, aching for more contact, and pressed open-mouthed kisses to her neck, his fingers plucking at the tips of her breasts.

Revelling in her soft mewls of pleasure, he continued to stroke her body into such flames of pleasure that she writhed against him, her body bucking insistently against his. He claimed her mouth once again, and one of his hands dipped low to catch the inside of her thighs. She whimpered and dug her nails into his biceps, clutching at him as his fingers played a symphony against her core.

For her part, Ekaterina could hardly understand what was happening between them. One minute she'd been admiring the gorgeous stranger, and the next she was being covered in his kisses! It was scandalous, terrifying and…absolutely wonderful. She knew she shouldn't be letting herself get carried away so completely, but she'd never felt desire so fiercely before. So she threw caution to the wind and let him sweep her away in sensation.

So lost were they in the heat of each other's touch that the cold lost its bite and all they knew was each other: each panted breath, each finger stroke, each clenched jaw.

Ekaterina could not stop trembling. Her nearly naked body was pressed up against this man's steely muscles. Dimly, she wondered what had got into her. How had this man so completely captivated her and overtaken her steely self-control? How had he penetrated all her defences?

And then he twisted his fingers, *just so*, and she lost all coherent thought completely.

Andrey could not believe what was happening. The most beautiful woman he had ever seen was warm putty in his artist's hands, her body bending and shuddering under his careful direction. Her plaintive cries were beautifully sweet—each a reward that added to his own pleasure.

Still, in a distant corner of his fogged mind he wondered…just who *was* she? He truly believed that no man could not be drawn to her, but how had they so instantly fallen into such a passionate embrace? How was it that he was already so intimately physical with her?

I don't care.

His questions dissolved into desire as he plied her with more and more kisses. Her dress was now over her bust, the offending material pushed away as he cupped one of her breasts with one hand and smoothed his palm up her stomach with his other. As she tightened her legs around his waist he imagined what he would do next.

He longed to rip away his own clothing and take her, right then and there in the forest, with no one but the geese to see. He wanted to push her into the tree and thrust himself deep while he watched her flushing face. He wanted to dig his fingers into her hips as he watched her head loll back with every rocking motion. Then he would spin her round and let her clutch blindly at the tree while he drove into her from behind, watching her arch and scream as they climaxed together.

Yes, he thought wildly. *Yes!*

He dropped his arms, reaching to fumble for the buttons on his trousers. She slid down his body, her feet dropping back to the snow-covered ground. Just as he managed to pull the top button loose, he felt her dainty hands on his. He pulled back to look her in the face. She was flushed pink, but her eyes were apologetic.

'No,' she said, shaking her head. 'I'm sorry.'

Andrey took two heaving breaths and sighed, leaning forward to plant a heavy hand on the trunk behind her.

'Why?' he groaned, closing his eyes.

* * *

Ekaterina awkwardly pulled down her dress and wrapped her coat tightly closed. She pursed her lips and looked away. Opposing emotions duelled within her. One part of her was thrilled and amazed at the sizzle of his lips, still warm on her skin. But the rational part of her was shocked and horrified. She was a noblewoman who prided herself on being different from the rest of the fickle courtiers—and yet here she was, throwing herself at a stranger.

'I don't understand this. And I don't know you,' she whispered, her feelings finding words.

He was silent and grim. It was true. The fire between them had been unexpected and inexplicable. On top of that, they *didn't* know one another. He didn't even know her name.

'Yet,' she said.

Her voice was small, but crystal clear. Andrey lifted his eyes to meet hers. Her expression was open. Earnest. Honest.

'No,' he agreed. 'Not yet.'

Ekaterina smiled then, and the lifting of her lips brightened her face. She cupped his cheek in her small hand, and he covered her fingers with his. The magnetism between them was undeniable. The echoes of their passion still pulsed under her skin. But she couldn't risk everything on a stranger—no matter how magnetic.

At least not yet.

She wanted to find some measure of happiness in the stifling court atmosphere, and perhaps he was her chance. There was obviously something that had drawn them together, be it destiny or chance. This man wasn't one of her aunt's tools, nor was he a candidate for a political marriage. So surely, *surely* he might enjoy her company and her body without ulterior motives. She desperately wanted to know him deeper, in soul and in body.

'Will you meet me again?' she asked, unable to keep the hopeful tone from her voice.

'Yes.'

A million times, yes, he added to himself.

She was a strange woman, he thought. But one worth pursuing. He didn't want to scare her away, so he didn't volunteer any more information about himself. Let her find out in due time, he decided.

She leaned into his willing embrace and pressed her ear to his chest. For a moment she listened to the steady beat of his heart.

He was an enigma, she thought. But he was as interesting as he was seductive. She didn't want him to abandon her, so she said nothing about her true identity. Let him believe she was a peasant girl on an equal footing, she decided.

She frowned. Let him wonder—except for one detail. 'My name,' she said, 'is Ekaterina.'

Chapter Two

The Winter Court was in full swing. Lavish drapery in silver and ivory hung from tall windows. Wreaths adorned with red and gold decorated every windowsill, and candles set in red glass spheres of varying sizes hung from the ornate ceiling. Court jesters clad in Christmas colours performed flips and cartwheels among the mingling courtiers dressed in all their finery.

And at the centre of it all, on a ridiculously gaudy throne on a raised platform, was the Empress Anna.

Ekaterina gritted her teeth as she glided through the hall, her golden fan clenched in a death grip and her lips a line of thinly veiled displeasure. This should have been a joyous Yuletide celebration. Oh, there were cakes shaped into Christmas trees and presents wrapped with shiny bows aplenty. And the spiced wine was flowing freely into greedy glasses. But still her aunt's tastes ran towards the vicious and distasteful.

In one corner of the magnificent hall stood a giant Christmas tree that was completely lit up with candles. But at the foot of that Christmas tree was a small group of nobles, dressed fabulously but walking about barefoot…on a thick carpet of sharp pine cones.

It was a punishment her aunt had thought up the night before, specifically for an aristocratic family that she felt had snubbed one of her current lovers. They grimaced and pretended to smile as the sharp edges of the dried cones pierced the tender soles of their feet, forced to pace as her aunt watched in morbid amusement.

And that was only the least of the macabre displays in the great hall.

Ekaterina bit her tongue and exhaled slowly, desperately trying to tamp down her rage at the indecent and cruel party amusements. It was wrong. It was horrible. It was definitely not behaviour worthy of an empress.

She chastised herself inwardly, gently tapping the tip of her closed fan against her chin. Such thoughts were dangerous. If ever voiced, those words would earn her not just humiliation but a secret and painful execution.

'My lady Ekaterina. You look absolutely beautiful tonight!'

At the sound of the voice Ekaterina turned suddenly,

her satin skirts swishing. An eligible aristocrat stood in front of her, his cheeks flushed with drink. He leered at her. She snapped her fan open, hiding her face. She knew his type. He was her aunt's favourite type of courtier: dumb, loud, money grubbing and abusive. He was after status and power, and he would do anything to rise in Empress Anna's favour.

'I'm sorry, Your Excellency…?' she said, arching an imperious brow.

'Please, call me Vladimir. I said you look beautiful,' he repeated with a grotesque smirk.

'Do I, Vladimir?' she asked, her tone superior.

'Yes, you look radiant,' he said, his lips smacking together hideously.

'Well, then,' Ekaterina said crisply, 'that's a shame, as you do not.'

With that she spun on her heel and marched away—only to be stopped a few seconds later by another tipsy social climber. Alternately ignoring and insulting her would-be suitors, Ekaterina slowly made her way to the edge of the room. She paused to press her gloved fingertips to her throbbing temples. She hated these royal functions; the decadence gave her a headache and the false smiles made her cheeks hurt. But most of all she hated, *hated* the fact that she was being dangled like a prize—a treat to reward the courtier who managed to impress her aunt the most.

Her jaw clenching, Ekaterina hazarded a glance over her shoulder.

Her aunt was doubled over in obscene guffaws of laughter as two miserable women—no doubt suspected of some trivial slight—were subjected to a humiliating face-painting. They were already smeared from head to toe with filth, and scraps of old food clung to their skin.

Ekaterina looked away, troubled and disgusted. Shaking her head, she edged nearer the exit and slipped around the ornate doors into the corridor. She quickly paced down the hall, lifting her skirts as she practically ran away.

Just a few moments, she told herself sternly. *I just need a little bit of air.*

Sure that her absence would be noted sooner rather than later, she quickly ducked around a corner—only to slam face first into a muscular chest. She looked up, eyes wide in panic.

'A-Andrey!' she stammered out in shock. 'What are you doing here?'

Andrey stared back at her, his jaw slack in surprise. Here was his mystery woman, his muse. But she no longer wore a simple cotton shift and a rough coat. Here she was, decked out in the most gorgeous finery, her hair up in ringlets and her face subtly painted according to the fashion of the day. She wore a simple yet elegant gown, with a gold satin corset top and full, voluminous skirts.

'Ekaterina,' he said, 'what are *you* doing here?'

'I'm...' She paused, her mind racing. She wasn't ready for him to find out who she really was. 'I've been forced to attend.'

'*Forced* to attend a Christmas ball?' he asked incredulously.

'Yes,' she rushed to say. 'I'm here for the Empress's amusement.'

Andrey's suspicions melted away into concern. Even he knew what type of amusements pleased the Empress. She was cruel to excess, and he despised her every smirk. He did not want to see his sweet Ekaterina fall prey to her sick games. No, he must not let her fall into the Empress's pudgy hands.

He took her by the hand and began to drag her away.

'Let's go,' he commanded briskly.

'To where?' she asked, trying to pull her hand from his. 'What do you think you are doing?'

'We have to get away from here,' he said grimly. 'You do *not* want to be at the Empress's mercy.'

'What?'

Frustrated by the strange turn of events, Ekaterina jerked backwards and pulled away sharply.

'What are you talking about?' she demanded.

Andrey took her by the shoulders and leaned in close, his green eyes darkly serious.

'You do not want to go to that ball,' he told her, squeezing her shoulders. 'When the Empress sees you... Sees how beautiful you are...' He paused and shuddered with revulsion. 'I won't let her use you for her twisted games. I won't let her hurt you.'

Andrey grabbed at her wrist, but Ekaterina kept her distance. Her eyes narrowed in thought. How did Andrey know of her aunt's demented behaviour?

'I thought you worked in the workshop,' she said slowly, her tone accusatory.

'I do,' he replied flatly as he took her hands in his. 'Now let's go.'

'No!' Ekaterina snapped angrily. 'Who are—?'

He stopped her with a kiss—and what a kiss it was!

He cupped her cheeks with his callused palms and pulled her close. His mouth covered hers, and his tongue and lips worked fiercely. Despite her misgivings, Ekaterina responded immediately, her angry words melting into a lusty sigh as Andrey plundered her mouth. She simply could not deny the hot wave of desire that flooded her senses when he touched her. She pressed in closer and tilted her head back farther, her lovely lashes fluttering.

* * *

Andrey dropped his hands to her waist and his lips to her smooth neck. He suckled at her earlobe and drew trails up the column of her neck with his tongue. She gasped and moaned as he lavished her with kisses, his hands searching her body.

And then he noticed it.

Her dainty hands were also exploring *his* body. Her fingers tentatively smoothed over his arms, down to his hands. Then they wandered over his chest and down his back. Slowly. Carefully. Shyly.

Andrey slowed his kisses to match her unhurried pace.

He just could not understand this woman, nor the hold she had over him. Why should he care about a peasant girl about to be devoured by the Empress's schemes? Why would he risk his own career for just one taste of her sweet sensuality?

Then she took his lower lip between her teeth, and he decided he couldn't care less.

Ekaterina revelled in Andrey's sweet caresses, her heart beating madly and her blood racing. Her suspicions grew dim in comparison to the heat rising in her stomach. As her mind grew foggy in the daze of pleasure, her instincts grew sharp. Despite her inexperience, she could not still her trembling fingers. Her hands roved over his body shamelessly, curiosity fuelling her exploration. Her hands dipped down past his hips, her fingers fanning over his taut thighs. Her thumb caught on one of the buttons at his crotch and Andrey let out a slow hiss.

Her interest piqued, she slowly brushed her thumb over the growing ridge in his trousers. His breathing hitched. Her lips curving over his, she pressed her open palm over the swelling there. It was hard and warm. She began to rub experimentally, and it quivered under her touch.

And when she squeezed, his thin ribbon of control broke.

He tangled his fingers in her hair and pulled her head back, his nose to her throat and his teeth scraping her skin.

Ekaterina stilled.

'Am I doing it wrong?' she asked uncertainly.

'No.' He grunted. *'No.'*

'Then…?'

He pulled her face to his and kissed her hard.

'You're driving me mad,' he groaned as he feathered kisses over her cheekbones.

'How?'

'You make me want to do things I can't do.'

Ekaterina pulled back slightly to meet his eyes. The sensual tension between them pulled taut.

'Like what?' she asked breathlessly.

He pushed her hand back over his throbbing, hungry

member, his larger hand covering hers. He leaned in close, his lips moving over her ear.

'I want to lift your skirts right here,' he told her in a harsh whisper. 'I want to rip away these beautiful clothes from your beautiful body. And I want to put *this* inside you.'

A shudder ran down Ekaterina's spine and her cheeks flushed scarlet. No noble would *dare* speak to her in such a way; none would not know her identity. Polished courtier he was not, and her doubts evaporated. She wanted to be with him; she wanted to know more about him. But she didn't want him to hate her for leading him on, for making him think she was no one important.

She frowned. If he found out she was more than a simple palace girl...if he found out she was the *niece* of the Empress...then he would think she was like all the other aristocrats—using and abusing those lower than themselves.

'Hey!'

Ekaterina stilled at the childish voice. She turned to see one of the friendlier servant girls calling to her from around a corner. The girl looked desperate and ready to run off at any second.

'She's looking for you!'

Ekaterina didn't need to be told who *she* was. She jumped away suddenly.

Gathering her skirts, she met Andrey's eyes.

'I'm sorry,' she explained. 'I've got to go. I'm *so* sorry.'

Andrey held out a hand but Ekaterina had already taken off, running. She had to make it back to the ballroom before her aunt got too impatient—or all her hard work being invisible would be for naught. She dashed into the great hall. Pushing past the drunken nobles, she skipped to a halt in front of her aunt's dais.

'Oh!' her aunt called excitedly. 'There you are, Ekaterina!'

'Yes, Empress,' she said with a deep curtsy.

'Come,' she said, beckoning with her pudgy fingers. 'Come meet my new friends.'

Friends? Ekaterina shivered involuntarily. She knew that her aunt had no real friends, only supporters and victims. The question was: which type were these?

'I found the most lovely man while I was in Italy,' Empress Anna said, giggling like a schoolgirl. 'An architect. I've commissioned him to complete the Hall of Light.'

She pulled a skinny man to the fore. He was elaborately dressed, his eyes darting about nervously.

'This,' she said proudly, 'is Bartolomeo Rastrelli.'

Ekaterina dipped her head in greeting.

'And he has the most brilliant apprentice,' Empress Anna continued. 'Where is he?' She looked around, mumbling his praises. 'Ah!' she called. '*There* he is.'

A man stepped through the crowd, and Ekaterina's heart stopped.

'This is my niece, the Lady Ekaterina Romanova,' Empress Anna announced to the men.

Her aunt's nasal voice faded as Ekaterina met the eyes of the architect's apprentice. She already knew this man—but evidently not as well as she had thought.

'Ekaterina,' the Empress said, 'this is Andrey Kvasov.'

Chapter Three

Ekaterina watched, dumbfounded, as Empress Anna placed a chubby hand on Andrey's shoulder. She could feel Andrey's glare, but her eyes were transfixed by the sight of her aunt's bejewelled hand sliding down to his chest. When the Empress gave him a quick pat, Ekaterina lifted steely, challenging eyes to his.

'It is an honour to finally meet you,' Ekaterina said politely, enunciating each word with aristocratic precision.

'Finally?' her aunt exclaimed. 'Have you also seen his magnificent work, Ekaterina?'

'Why, yes, indeed,' Ekaterina replied, her tone slightly sardonic. 'I have seen his great *skill* in action in a *very* different setting. But I never thought he'd been applying his skills elsewhere, my honoured aunt.'

'If I'd known I'd been courting such a *noble* audience, I can promise you that I would have given you due respect, my lady,' Andrey stated, his voice flat.

Ekaterina lifted her chin, her eyes cold.

'You don't seem to be a fan of Andrey's work,' her aunt commented blithely. 'Were you not impressed?'

'It wasn't worth remembering,' Ekaterina said with a bitter slant to her lips.

A crease formed in her aunt's brow. She turned to the architect's apprentice and patted his arm affectionately.

'Don't take my niece's words to heart, Andrey,' she said reassuringly. 'She's an excellent girl, but she has little taste for the finer things of life. Why, just look at that shabby dress!'

Empress Anna laughed at her own joke, oblivious to the heated glares passing between the two people near her.

'Now, go,' Anna said, nudging Andrey's shoulder. 'Get me a drink, will you, my dear?'

His cold eyes sliding away, Andrey strode from the throne and into the crowd. As soon as he was out of earshot, Anna turned to Ekaterina with a conspiratorial wink.

'Well, isn't he quite the catch?' she said with a suggestive waggle of her fat brows.

Ekaterina inclined her head, careful not to disagree but also not to show too much interest. Emotions were dangerous at court. Even so, she discreetly followed Andrey with appraising eyes. In fact, it was hard not to notice him, as he stood at least a head taller than most of the people in the hall. But his height wasn't even his most striking feature. He was magnificent, with his thick shock of dark hair, his broad shoulders and his tapered waist. He was the picture of masculine perfection; yes, he was the perfect catch.

Manipulative, social-climbing fool, Ekaterina thought bitterly.

'He will do well at court,' she mused aloud.

'Yes,' her aunt agreed with a sniff. 'Especially after I take him as a lover.'

'I thought he was meant to be working here as an architect,' Ekaterina said, trying to sound uninterested.

'Oh, he's already been instrumental in designing many parts of the palace. But I'm sure Rastrelli will be able to spare him now and again,' the Empress replied with an indifferent shrug. 'Besides, he couldn't do better, really.'

'No,' Ekaterina murmured quietly. 'He really couldn't.'

After all, how could the niece of an empress compare to the Empress herself? Despite her determination to remain aloof, Ekaterina felt her throat constrict. She blinked back the mist in her eyes. It hurt, she admitted to herself. It hurt more than she could have imagined.

Aunt and niece watched as Andrey walked through

the crowd with purpose, neither turning to the right nor the left. He didn't even pause, except when a beautiful young noblewoman stopped him by putting her dainty hand on his arm. He turned slightly as she drew closer, her thick lashes fluttering. Andrey's expression didn't change; his facial muscles were like stone.

But the Empress was not amused.

Ekaterina had to resist the urge to take a step away as her aunt's face grew nearly purple with rage. The Empress stepped forward, her chest heaving and a short finger pointed accusingly at the unsuspecting noblewoman.

'You!' she shrieked, her voice piercing. 'Come here this instant!'

The noblewoman froze, her head slowly turning to face Anna, terror vivid in her eyes.

'Yes, you,' her aunt bellowed maliciously. 'Move!'

The poor woman picked up her skirts and scurried forward. She hastened to kneel, her head bobbing up and down in a desperate apology.

'Your Majesty,' she stammered, frightened out of her wits. 'Please forgive me. I had no idea he was of any interest—'

'Silence!' Empress Anna demanded. 'You grovel like a pig.'

'Empress, please—'

But Empress Anna stamped her foot, cutting her off.

She lifted the hem of her dress, exposing the toe of one of her shiny shoes.

'Apologise,' she hissed angrily.

'A thousand apologies, my—'

'Not with your mouth, with your tongue,' the Empress commanded with a sadistic grin. 'Lick my shoes clean, you cow.'

Trembling, the pitiful woman got down on all fours and began to lick the Empress's shoes, to the accompaniment of feigned laughter all around. Horrified, Ekaterina took the opportunity to slowly back away, not wanting to witness any more cruelty for the day. She knew her aunt would entertain herself with such cruel *divertissements* for a long time yet…and her presence would quickly be forgotten. So Ekaterina quietly slipped from the hall, ready to retire to her chambers to nurse her bruised ego and conflicting emotions.

But just as she turned into the royal wing of the palace she felt a hand latch on to her wrist. She spun away, glaring. It was Andrey, his eyes fierce and demanding. He rounded on her, backing her into the wall and placing both hands beside her head.

'You were toying with me, lady,' he growled.

'*I* was toying with *you*?' Ekaterina blurted out angrily. 'You are the one set on advancing your rank by seducing the Empress!'

'What are you talking about?' Andrey exclaimed.

'As if you didn't know,' Ekaterina accused, jabbing a finger into his muscled chest. 'You will be the Empress's new pet, won't you!'

'Her pet?' He leaned in close so that their noses were almost touching. 'So says the Winter Court's *sweetheart*.'

'I should have known better than to trust you,' Ekaterina said, her voice trembling. 'You got what you wanted from me, didn't you? You sampled the wares but then hooked a bigger, better fish. I suppose you won't be needing to seduce me any longer, now that you've got into the Empress's good graces.'

Ekaterina turned away, blinking rapidly. Andrey frowned. Her eyes were bright with unshed tears. Her lower lip was faintly quavering.

But why?

It struck him suddenly, like a blow to the chest, and he nearly staggered backwards. Of course, he realised, she hadn't known his identity and he hadn't known hers. He covered his eyes with one hand. It had been one massive misunderstanding.

But before he could gather his wits to compose himself, Ekaterina pushed away from him with a choked cry and fled down the hall. He watched her go, his hands hanging heavily at his sides. Then he slowly turned away, a mournful expression on his face.

Soon the hall was empty again, until one of the Empress's maids stepped out from behind a curtain, a wicked glint in her eye.

Chapter Four

They were out riding, all three of them plus a retinue of courtiers. The snow was soft underneath their horses' hooves and the air was sharp. Ekaterina sat stiffly atop her mare, her back ramrod straight and her face neutral. She hadn't wanted to come, but it would have been impossible to refuse the summons of the Empress. Thankfully, they were on their way back to the palace now. Her aunt rode beside her, a strange smile playing about her lips. Andrey rode behind, his face sullen and brooding.

A fine trio.

'So, my dear niece,' the Empress began, her tone conversational, 'how have you been lately? I haven't seen much of you since you arrived at court.'

'Thank you for your concern, Aunt,' Ekaterina replied. 'I have—'

'By the way,' her aunt interrupted brusquely. 'Did you hear what happened to Sergei? The baker?'

'I didn't realise you knew him,' Ekaterina said lightly. 'He is a good baker.'

'Was.'

Ekaterina blinked and tried to remain calm.

'Was, Aunt?'

The Empress sniffed delicately.

'He was sent to Siberia yesterday,' her aunt informed her. 'Because he was caught stealing bread for his family.'

Ekaterina's throat closed.

'And his family?'

'Thrown to the street, as they well deserved.'

Ekaterina felt numb. The poor man and his family. She would have to instruct her own servants to find the family, give them money and hopefully help them find some means of living. Unfortunately she could no longer help Sergei.

'Do you know what that means, Ekaterina, dear?' her aunt queried.

'That his family will probably perish in the cold?'

'Yes—but no.' Her aunt clicked her tongue. 'That's not the lesson here, my dear.'

The Empress reined in her horse, wheeling it round

so that it blocked the path. She looked from Ekaterina to Andrey and then back again, her eyes narrowing.

'The lesson is that stealing will be punished harshly,' Anna said calmly. 'No matter who the culprit is.'

She let an awkward silence blanket the group before kicking her horse into a trot.

'Remember that, both of you.'

Ekaterina didn't dare look back to gauge Andrey's reaction. It was clear that the warning was meant for them, but why? Her stomach tightened at the memories of them in the field, in the corridor and in the royal wing. Someone had seen. Someone had whispered. And now they were both on thin ice.

When they reached the palace Ekaterina ignored Andrey and dismounted gracefully. She handed the reins to the stable keeper and bowed deeply before escaping her aunt's oppressive presence. She wandered the echoing corridors aimlessly, her mind whirring.

Danger on one side and unrequited attraction on the other. How she wanted to return to the country, to be with her loving family once again!

'My lady!' a page called to her.

Ekaterina halted and waited for the breathless page to reach her. The boy bowed and presented her with a scroll.

'A missive, my lady,' he said as she took the letter. 'From the architect's apprentice, Andrey Kvasov.'

Ekaterina nearly dropped the letter. *The fool!* She slid the scroll into her sleeve, feigning complete indifference.

'You may go,' she said, waving the boy away.

As soon as he was out of sight she pulled the letter from her sleeve and unravelled it hurriedly. The words were hastily but beautifully scrawled...and they would damn them both if they were seen by another other eyes.

'My lady,' the missive read, 'I must explain. Please come to my suite.'

She crumpled the paper in her hands, her ire boiling over. Jaw set, she stalked to the western wing of the palace. She knew where he was staying; she'd had one of her guards investigate. Without knocking, she threw open the doors to Andrey's suite and slammed them shut behind her. Andrey jumped up from his seat.

'You!' she shouted angrily as she stormed towards him. 'What were you thinking?'

She shook the ragged letter in the air, and then pitched it into the fireplace. It dissolved in a bright burst of flame.

'I needed to see you,' Andrey explained, his palms up.

'Could you not think of a way that doesn't involve us both getting killed?'

'What on earth are you talking about?'

Ekaterina stared at him incredulously.

'Haven't you realised the Empress plans to make you

hers?' she asked disbelievingly. 'Are you unaware that all your *hard work* has finally paid off?'

A look of abject horror passed over Andrey's usually stoic face. Then, finally, understanding dawned on him and he grew calm. He relaxed his stance and took a slow step forward.

'I see,' he said in a low, almost gentle tone. 'Did you think I'd planned to be the object of her affection?'

Ekaterina's brow creased, confusion mounting alongside her anger.

'Of course you had! Why else would you be at court?' Her voice quietened. 'Why else would you lure ladies into your grasp?'

'You are mistaken, my lady,' he corrected sternly. 'I am here as an apprentice to plan and construct the Hall of Light.'

'Ha!' Ekaterina exclaimed in disbelief, her voice bitter. 'You are like every other man here,' she accused. 'You prey on—'

In three quick strides Andrey was across the room and a hair's breadth away from her. His hands closed over hers tightly. He captured her eyes with his and her voice faded away in surprise.

'You are *wrong*,' he said, his voice low but intense. 'You have been at court for far too long, my lady.'

'You used me,' Ekaterina said flatly, her eyes hard.

Andrey shook his head and pulled her closer, setting her palms on his chest so that she could feel his wildly beating heart.

'I had no such ambitions,' he said seriously. 'I thought you were a peasant girl. I had no idea you were royalty. In fact, when I found out who you were I thought you were the one using me.'

Ekaterina was silent as she searched his face for any hint of duplicity. But his face, though not expressive, was free of any of the telltale signs of dishonesty. Her brows lifted. He was right; neither of them had known who the other was. It was possible that he had wanted her for herself. It was *possible*. So...

'So,' she said slowly, 'you do not want to be the Empress's lover?'

'I could never touch that sadistic woman,' he said gravely. 'Never.'

Then he carefully took Ekaterina's chin between his thumb and forefinger and tilted her face up to his. His eyes roved her perfect face, from her pouting lips to her earnest eyes. She was beautiful, and in more than just her physical appearance. She was a noblewoman who spurned courtly ways, who decried the idea of using love as a weapon and who wanted nothing more than honesty. He'd never met anyone like her before; she was a pearl amongst wooden beads.

Yes, she was beautiful.

Andrey carefully lowered his lips to her cheek, his breath ghosting over her lashes. She swallowed nervously, and his lips curved at the innocence that lay beneath her sharp mouth—a mouth he would very much like to savour once again.

'I will never be her lover,' he murmured against her cheek. 'But I might like to be yours.'

Ekaterina started in surprise, but Andrey held her fast. Her heart raced and blood rushed to her ears. She was sure she had not heard him right.

'Say that again?' she whispered.

He smiled and nuzzled her cheek, his stubble gently scratching her delicate skin as he dipped lower to nibble at the corner of her lips.

'I could be *your* lover,' he repeated, his voice low and seductive.

With the tip of his index finger, he traced a line from her collarbone to the swell of her breast. She shivered under the feather-light touch. But still she hesitated.

'But what if my aunt—?'

'Let's not speak of her right now,' Andrey told her, his hands tangling in her hair.

'But she—'

Andrey swept her objections away by pulling her into a deep kiss, his lips rough on hers.

Ekaterina melted into his embrace, letting him plunder

her mouth and relishing the warm ache that was building between her thighs. Her thoughts grew hazy with pleasure as his tongue delved deeply into her mouth, pushing past the wall of her teeth and sweeping her into a delicious dance.

She was barely aware of the workings of his skilful hands until she felt her bodice drop to the floor. She had no time to be surprised, however, as he continued his onslaught. The cotton of her underdress seemed rough against her skin as he moulded his hands to her ample chest, rubbing in an arousing circular motion. Her breathing hitched, and she cried out in delight as he gently pinched the erect peaks.

Fingers twisting in the fabric of his loose shirt, she pulled herself closer to his heat, breaking off their kiss to rest her chin over his shoulder.

Andrey was merciless in courting Ekaterina's passion, his hands sliding down her back to cup her bottom. As he elicited another moan from his willing partner he planned his method of attack.

He would rip away her skirts and push her gently to the lush carpets below. Then, while holding her gaze, he would slowly enter her. He would watch her face change, and then he would bring her to such heights of pleasure that she would come, screaming his name to the ceiling.

Burning in anticipation, he sank down to his knees before her, smiling as she tangled her fingers in his thick hair. She seemed confused at the sudden loss of contact, but it was soon forgotten as he glanced up to meet her curious blue eyes.

Puzzled, Ekaterina stared down at his chiselled features. But then his fingers found the lacings of her skirt and her heart jumped. Andrey was so tall that even on his knees he was at eye level with her bosom—a fact that suddenly made her flush. It had not gone unnoticed. Andrey smiled devilishly and slowly pressed his nose between her two pert breasts. His fingers worked the closures of her skirts as he began to suckle her through her thin undershirt. Ekaterina threw her head back, her mouth opening to cry out.

Then a familiar voice suddenly cut all activity short.

'Andrey, my darling!' her aunt called out from down the hall, her booming voice adopting a playful, singsong quality. 'I've come for a visit!'

The lovers jumped apart and stared at each other in near panic. The Empress was only moments away from Andrey's suite.

'What are we to do?' Ekaterina asked in fright. 'She will kill you if she finds me here.' Her hands fluttered wildly over her chest. 'And my family! What will she do to them?'

* * *

Andrey took a split second to savour the sight of a noblewoman worrying for others before herself. Ekaterina was indeed exceedingly rare and precious. He felt himself fall just a little bit further under her spell. But now was not the time to dawdle in admiration—not when the monster was about to pound on his door.

'Quick,' he told her in a calm whisper, 'follow me.'

He grabbed Ekaterina's discarded bodice in one hand and took her by the arm with the other. He guided her to the fireplace and knelt beside it. Letting go of Ekaterina's hand, he placed his open palms on one of the gilded wall panels, his fingers slowly roving over the raised decorations.

'What are you doing?' Ekaterina demanded in an angry whisper.

She looked over her shoulder as her aunt began to pound on the door.

'Are you decent, my darling?' the Empress called. 'I'm coming in!'

'I'll show you things that only architects realise,' Andrey said, flashing her a confident grin.

His nimble fingers found what they were looking for. He pressed one raised circle with his thumb and the panel sprang open with a click, revealing a small secret passageway. He pulled Ekaterina down and helped her crawl into the space before getting in himself and pulling the panel closed. It was not a moment too soon as they heard the Empress barrel into the suite a second later.

They didn't stay to hear her swearing.

Instead, they forged on. The space gradually widened, revealing a very narrow hall. There was barely space for the two of them, so they had to walk in single file. There was hardly any light, and they carefully felt their way along.

'Where does it go?' Ekaterina asked in a whisper.

'If I had to guess,' Andrey murmured speculatively, 'I'd bet this widens even farther and joins up with other secret passages. We could probably go anywhere from here. Where do you want to exit?'

'The kitchens,' Ekaterina replied immediately. 'The servants there would never betray me.'

'Let me lead,' Andrey suggested, catching her wrist.

Ekaterina nodded in agreement and paused, turning to the side and flattening her back against the wall to make room for him to pass. Andrey began to slide by, but stopped suddenly. They were sandwiched between two walls, their chests nearly touching.

'Now, this is familiar,' Andrey murmured, amused.

'Oh?' Ekaterina arched a brow. 'I don't recall being stuck in a secret passageway before.'

Andrey smirked. Danger was both behind and in front of them, and yet this fierce young woman had the audacity to joke. He felt desire spike down his thighs. The fact that they were skating on the very edge of disaster only fuelled his need to touch her. He slid his palms down her hips and cupped the undersides of her thighs. He pulled her up so her legs were tight around his waist and her back pressed against the wall.

'Not the place,' he said in a low growl. 'The position.'

'Ah, yes,' Ekaterina answered with a small smile. 'I remember now. What were we doing again?'

'Let me remind you.'

Andrey kissed her slowly, his lips moving lazily against hers. But his fingers were quick, deftly pulling at the laces keeping her skirt tight around her waist. Ekaterina experimentally rolled her hips against his, smiling when she elicited a low grunt of approval. It was a dangerous game they were playing, and the tension only heightened her senses.

It seemed an eternity before Andrey took a minuscule step back, letting her slide down his chest before offering her a cheeky smile.

'Ready now?'

He stepped forward along the passageway, but as soon as she began to follow, her overskirt dropped in a heap to the ground. Andrey glanced over his shoulder, a wicked gleam in his eye. Ekaterina grinned, accepting the unspoken challenge. They made their way slowly though the maze of passages, breathing more easily when it wid-

ened into a narrow corridor with skylights above to light
the way. It truly was an intricate system, and Ekaterina
could almost see Andrey mapping it out in his head.

That simply would not do.

They rounded a bend in the passage and Ekaterina
suddenly shoved Andrey into the wall, her eyes shining.
She grabbed him by the lapels of his shirt and pulled him
down for a searing kiss. He responded in kind, grabbing
at her plain shift. But Ekaterina would not be outdone;
her small hands worked furiously at the buttons of his
shirt. She pulled the offending material away, exposing his sculpted abdomen. Her hands wandered over his
chest and then over his shoulders and down his arms.
The shirt fell to the floor.

And then she pulled away. She looked him over once
and then turned and flounced away. Andrey groaned
and followed her determinedly.

He caught her at a short flight of stairs, grabbing her
by the waist and kissing her from behind. He spun them
around and sat, pulling her down so that she was strad-
dling his knees. He laved her neck with kisses while
pushing up her underskirts and grabbed her bottom,
pulling her flush against his heat. With one hand holding her fast, he pushed up her undershirt and cupped a
breast. He teased the erect peak with his tongue, smirk-
ing when she undulated above him, lost in the sensation.

He took the opportunity to quickly pull her shirt over

her head and toss it down the stairs. He met her playful glare with a grin—now they were both half naked. He wore only his trousers, and she her underskirt. He stood, helping her to her feet.

'Almost there.' He smiled.

She inclined her head, the double meaning not lost on her. They continued on their way, their fingers loosely entwined. Every now and again they would cast each other lascivious glances. Ekaterina grew bold, her jaunty gait causing her pert breasts to bounce ever so slightly with every step. Andrey's nostrils flared with desire, and he unobtrusively flexed his arm and chest muscles while walking...which made Ekaterina stare openly, her jaw slightly slack.

Their game of seduction continued...until they turned a corner to face a final door.

'I think this is the door to the corridor leading to the kitchens,' Andrey said, placing his hand against the thick panel.

He turned to Ekaterina, his eyes serious.

'Shall we finish this?' he asked.

'We can't go outside like this,' Ekaterina said, gesturing to their lack of clothes.

'That wasn't what I was talking about.'

Andrey pulled her close, his hands slowly travelling down the length of her body until they reached the waistband of her underskirt. His eyes locked on hers, he slowly pushed the skirt down, leaving her last piece of clothing to pool at her feet. Then he stepped away. She blushed beautifully as he slowly looked her up and down, the lusty admiration in his eyes as plain as day. She wanted to raise her arms to cover herself, but resisted the urge. *Let him look,* she thought resolutely.

But Andrey didn't just want to look. He closed the distance between them and began showering her with heady kisses. His lips travelled from her face to her neck, then to her bare shoulders. He slowly sank to his knees, worshipping every available inch of her body with his tongue and lips. He painted a story of desire on her body; he was the artist and she was his canvas.

Ekaterina sighed in pleasure, lost for words. Her heart swelled with emotion. Outside, their love was forbidden, and if anyone even saw them exchange a knowing look their lives would be in danger. But here, and only here, they were safe, hidden away in their own private passageway. And so Ekaterina gave herself over to their shared passion, indulging in these few moments they had together. After all, who knew when they would be so free again?

When finally Andrey paused to look up, she was flushed with pleasure, her skin tingling and moist. She eased down to kneel with him and covered his face with soft kisses.

'Is it my turn now?' she asked playfully, pulling away.

Delight lit Andrey's face, and he slowly stood. He reached for the buckles on his trousers, but Ekaterina batted his hands away and pulled them open herself. With a quick tug his trousers hit the floor and he sprang free—tall, thick and pulsing with desire. Curiosity overwrote modesty and Ekaterina slowly reached out to touch the bulging tip with a fingertip. She slowly covered his shaft with her palm. Then she experimentally pumped her hand, stroking the velvet skin. Andrey nearly doubled over.

Ekaterina watched as he swelled even more, the taut flesh growing even harder under her touch. But before she could do more, Andrey caught her wrist and pulled her up.

'Not yet,' he grunted. 'I've not finished with you yet.'

His mouth was hot on hers, and he pulled her naked body flush against his. He delighted in her passionate sighs and her sweet scent before gently lowering her to her back on the ground. His fingers drew a tantalising path from her chin, stopping to tweak her caramel peaks before circling her navel. Hooking one of her legs over his shoulder, he tenderly planted soft kisses to the underside of her knee, up her inner thigh. Her breathing hitched, her scent becoming heady with need.

Murmuring mindless reassurances, Andrey dipped one long finger lower, coating it in her sweet nectar before sliding it inside her core. Ekaterina twisted in pleasure, her back arching off the floor. Andrey slowly withdrew and then pushed back in, his thumb rubbing small, coaxing circles around the pearl of her body as he did so. When she began to buck in wild, passionate abandon he pulled his fingers away.

Her complaining cry quickly turned into a low moan of pleasure as he positioned himself above her, his tip at her entrance. Bracing himself against the floor, he pushed himself in slowly, marvelling at how she constricted around him. She grabbed blindly for his shoulders, her nails digging into his muscled back as he began to thrust. His breathing grew ragged as he upped his pace, and Ekaterina began to writhe in pleasure beneath him.

They were close, so close…and then there were voices from outside the panel.

They stopped suddenly, eyes whipping round to the panel. Though muffled, they could both hear the sound of maids talking, their voices growing louder as they drew near. Ekaterina was about to slide away from Andrey when she felt him cover her mouth with his large hand.

'We're not done, my lady,' he murmured. 'But you must be quieter.'

She was about to protest, but he resumed his fervent rocking and her eyes rolled back instead. Their bodies came together with the sharp slap of skin on skin, and Ekaterina could barely focus on keeping the bubbling scream of pleasure down. Her body hummed with ecstasy, and she bit down on the heel of his palm to keep from crying out.

And still the voices grew louder.

Andrey stared down at her with his bright green eyes, his thrusts never wavering. His jaw grew tight and his rhythm grew frantic. He leaned closer, his other hand anchoring her hip to the floor and his eyes promising something more. Their breathing came in short gasps, sweat glistening on their skin.

Finally the voices faded out of earshot.

Andrey pulled his hand away, grabbed her hips with both hands and plunged in so deep that they both screamed in bliss, their voices echoing down the secret corridors. The world exploded in light and pleasure as they rode out the high together, toes curled and backs arched. Finally spent, they collapsed limply in a tangle of moist limbs, Ekaterina's thighs quivering around his hips.

It seemed an eternity before they could manage the strength to stand, and they had to hold each other tight to ward off the sudden chill.

Ekaterina began to giggle, ensconced in Andrey's muscular arms. He turned a sceptical eye on her and she laughed outright.

'We can't go out like this!' she said again.

'Well,' Andrey said reasonably, 'I suppose we'll just have to make our way back to my suite.'

'Collecting our clothes like breadcrumbs on a trail?'

'Yes,' he said, nodding sagely. 'I suppose so.'

They picked themselves up and slowly made their way back through the tunnels, donning the clothes they had abandoned along the way. They teased and kissed as young lovers would, relishing the amorous attention. It was sweet. It was lovely.

But it couldn't last.

Ekaterina only allowed herself to realise that fact much later, when she was safely back in her royal suite, alone with her thoughts. No, she told herself, they would never be safe to be together as long as they were under her aunt's thumb. Andrey was in danger. Her whole family was in danger.

But there was one thing she could do.

Ekaterina pulled out paper and ink. Dipping her quill into the inkwell, she formulated a plan. And then she began to write.

Chapter Five

It was Christmas Eve, and the Empress was hosting a grand ball in the newly unveiled Hall of Light. Ekaterina wandered through the crowd of guests, completely surrounded yet completely alone. She didn't really mind. She was content to bask in the beauty of the fruition of Andrey's planning and hard work—his ultimate creation.

During their few and precious stolen moments together he had alternated between lavishing her with sensuality and describing his ongoing project. Rastrelli had given him free rein, and Andrey had created this pinnacle of beauty in the Catherine Palace. Ekaterina's heart swelled with pride; this hall would be a place remembered for generations to come.

True to its moniker, the hall glowed golden with reflected light. The walls and ceilings were covered in mirrors, each framed in polished gold. Golden chandeliers hung from the ceiling, and the floor was of two-tone marble. It was a masterpiece of architecture.

Ekaterina aimlessly admired each gilded frame, unique yet unified in design, and marvelled at the attention to detail. Besides, it distracted her from the spectacle at the other end of the hall.

Her aunt sat poised on a golden throne, and Andrey was seated on a cushioned stool to her right. Ekaterina tried to avoid sneaking glances their way, only slightly mollified by Andrey's stiff composure. She gritted her teeth and turned away once again as her aunt continued to fawn all over him. She couldn't be angry with him, since neither really had a choice in the matter. When the Empress called for his company, he had no choice but to attend to her. So far he'd been able to fend off her amorous advances, but there was no telling when her aunt would tire of the endless game.

Meanwhile, at the head of the Hall of Light, Andrey was fighting the urge to slap the Empress's hand away. She was clinging to him once again, and he felt nothing but revulsion for this woman who so tormented her subjects. But there were niceties to be observed in order to stay alive, so he managed a few tight smiles and curt nods to satisfy her.

Out of the corner of his eye, he caught sight of a woman.

Ekaterina.

She was clad in a stunning scarlet gown trimmed with gold, her midnight hair tumbling freely over her pale shoulders. He subtly followed her movement across the hall, watching as she paused before each of his individually inspired creations. Sometimes she would reach out to run a fingertip over the design, her blue eyes awed. It gratified him to watch her admiring his work, making the evening somewhat bearable.

The musicians suddenly struck up a familiar tune. The guests hurriedly rushed to take up dancing positions at either end of the hall.

Ah, Andrey thought, *here is my chance.*

He stood and offered his hand to the Empress.

'Would you care to dance, Empress?' he invited with a bow.

'Oh, no,' she answered with a pout and a dismissive wave of her hand. 'I prefer to watch these types of things.'

Of course you do, he thought rather uncharitably. *You can hardly walk since gorging yourself silly.*

'Then let me entertain you,' he said instead.

Andrey hurried to take up a dancing spot, trying not to appear overly eager to get away. He caught Ekaterina's eye from across the hall, where she had also sneaked into position. He risked a quick wink. And then the dance began.

It took a while for them to reach each other, but when they finally did they enjoyed a few moments of sheer bliss. Their eyes met, their hands touched and they swayed around the ballroom, all of a sudden in a world of their own. Andrey discreetly bent forward to brush his lips across the shell of her ear, clasping her fingers tightly in his. She smiled as they shared a lingering look…and then the moment was over as the song ended.

Ekaterina dropped gracefully into a deep curtsy, acknowledging Andrey's formal bow with a slight tilt of her dainty chin.

Andrey could not look away, much less step back. He knew he should return to the Empress's side; he knew he should tear his eyes away; he *knew* he was courting trouble just by being within a few feet of the Empress's niece. But, with an electric tingle singing in his ears, he dared to take a step forward instead of back.

Ekaterina's head shot up, a clear warning in her worried eyes. Andrey simply shook his head and held out a hand…just as the band began to play another waltz. Ekaterina hesitantly stepped back into his embrace, pressing her slender fingers into his palm. He whirled her around the room in time to the music, his heart pounding in his ears. He ached to pull her closer, but etiquette dictated that they keep their distance as they danced. And so he focused on her tiny hand in his and on the feel of her arm lightly resting on his shoulder as they swayed to the sweet music.

His eyes traced the gleam of her hair, the elegant sweep of her pale neck and the slight heave of her chest. He wondered if she was feeling the same rush of adrenaline and desire that he was. He risked a glance at her face; she was flushed, her eyes bright. He smirked.

'Ekaterina,' he murmured under his breath, 'do you see the mirrors between the windows?'

She glanced around and gave him a quick nod. There were large oblong mirrors edged in gold all around the hall.

'I want you to look straight at them all. What do you see?'

Ekaterina frowned, her eyes darting from mirror to mirror. It was strange...when she looked head-on into each mirror she didn't see herself. No, instead she saw the reflection of part of the ceiling. *How odd,* she thought to herself. She wondered if Andrey had tilted the mirrors to accentuate the light.

'The ceiling?' she whispered back.

'What in the ceiling?'

Ekaterina's brows knotted as she tried to focus on the reflection in each mirror. Each was exactly the same. Her eyes widened as recognition dawned.

Every mirror reflected a golden sculpture of lovers entwined in a sweet embrace. But it wasn't just any pair of lovers; no, she saw her own face in the golden statuette. Hers and his. Andrey had immortalised their secret kiss in the ceiling of the Hall of Light.

Ekaterina could not contain her gasp of surprise and delight.

'What have you done?' she breathed, feeling both flattered and terrified.

'I have made us untouchable,' he replied quietly, meeting her eyes defiantly. 'And you will always remember what we have together when you come to the Hall of Light.'

'You daring, clever fool,' she whispered. 'You take too many risks!'

But even as Ekaterina reprimanded him she felt a surge of exhilaration and desire course through her veins. She considered his square, determined jawline and his serious eyes. She wanted to show him how much she appreciated this clever gesture of devotion, this subtle rebellion against the Empress. But what could she do? Certainly not a kiss, nor a hug. Perhaps…

Her heart swelling, Ekaterina squeezed his hand. Then, with the hand that lay on his shoulder, she slid her palm up so that she could gently stroke his neck with the tips of her fingers.

Andrey stifled a groan and a shudder. It wasn't much, but this brief illicit touch in the centre of the Hall of

Light gave him strength—strength enough, perhaps, to survive the night.

At least that was what he believed—until Empress Anna rose and clapped her hands, ending the dance abruptly. The courtiers spun to a halt, all eyes on the Empress. A feeling of dread knotted in Andrey's stomach as he watched her rise from her chair, a cruel smirk lifting her lips. She beckoned to him with one curling finger, and he fought the urge to stay rooted to his spot. But the Empress was not one to be openly defied, so he begrudgingly headed back towards the dais.

As soon as he reached her side she looped her hand through his elbow and addressed the waiting crowd.

'Christmas is upon us,' she announced, her voice echoing in the hall. 'And I have an extra special treat for all of you today. As you know, my niece has recently joined my Winter Court, and she is still unmarried.'

The Empress paused to fix her rival with a malicious smirk.

Ekaterina suddenly felt light-headed, as if she were floating away. She stared up at her aunt, eyes wide in shock and dismay.

'Aunt,' she announced, forcing her voice not to tremble, 'I believe I shall retire for the evening. Please excuse me.'

'Now, now,' her aunt said disapprovingly. 'You're going to play my game whether you like it or not, my dear!'

Empress Anna snapped her fingers and a line of aristocratic bachelors marched out onto the dais in single file. Ekaterina's throat closed in dread. She knew all of these men by name. Captain Boris Zukov, a ruthless military man. Count Vitaly, who had once beaten a servant to the verge of death for dropping a cup. Igor of the North, known for torturing his mistresses once he tired of them. Her ribs felt like constricting bands of steel as she took in the sight of each cruel, malicious man.

These are my suitors, she realised as panic shredded her stomach.

Anna grabbed Andrey's sleeve and leaned her cheek against his. Her breath was hot and rancid against his skin.

'Let this be a lesson to you, foolish boy,' she muttered under her breath. '*No one* steals from me and gets away with it unscathed.'

Andrey felt frozen in place, as if he might be shattered by his hammering heart. His eyes found Ekaterina, whose face had gone blank.

'My dearest niece, you have been dallying among the wildflowers for too long. So I have assembled this group of suitable men for you,' her aunt bellowed. 'I demand that you choose a husband from these suitors by the end of tomorrow's Christmas celebrations.'

To be shackled to one of these barbarians...

'Aunt,' Ekaterina protested, 'surely—'

'If you don't choose a husband,' she warned, interrupting, 'I will choose for you and send you, married, back to your father's house tomorrow night.' She paused, her smile sharp. 'And if I have to send my favourite niece away I don't believe I will very much care for this bright room any longer. Nor the man who designed it.'

The thinly veiled threat hung in the air between the lovers. She was to be condemned to a life of violence and servitude no matter what—and if she did not willingly walk into that trap, the Empress would damn them both.

Chapter Six

~~~~~~~~~~~~~~~~~~~~~~~

The next day came far too quickly. After the events of the Christmas Eve ball, the palace had been buzzing with gossip. Some pitied Ekaterina's fate while others sniffed and basked in her misfortune. But all were excitedly guessing at which suitor she would choose.

All, that was, except for Andrey.

Andrey had spent most of the night pacing, his mind awhirl. After Empress Anna's announcement he hadn't been permitted a moment alone with Ekaterina. Instead, he had been rudely ushered from the hall as his mentor, Rastrelli, had erupted in panicked appeal. His last stolen glance had been of Ekaterina's pale, stone-faced expression as she surveyed her potential husbands.

Now, finally released from his suite by the Empress's

personal guard, he walked briskly into the reception hall of the palace, where a Christmas Day luncheon was being served. But as he strode into the room he was nearly shoved out of the way by a burly nobleman, barrelling past. He blinked, surprised. It was Count Vitaly—and he was as red as a ripe tomato and swearing profusely.

Frowning, Andrey entered the grand hall and was greeted by the hushed whispers of the Winter Court. He glanced up at the royal dais. The Empress was beet-red and glowering down...at Ekaterina.

But when he peered at Ekaterina through the throng of milling nobles, his frown only deepened. She was not her usual serious, serene self. No, the young woman was tittering and giggling behind a gold-feathered fan as she openly flirted with her two remaining suitors, Captain Boris Zukov and Igor of the North.

Andrey circled the edges of the ballroom, studying the strange, sly smile that lifted the corners of her ruby-red lips. Her lusty allure was on full display as she laid her fingers on Captain Zukov's arm while tiptoeing to whisper something in Igor's ear. The men were captivated by her...except when they paused to glare at each other over her head.

Ekaterina caught a glimpse of Andrey's stormy face from the corner of her eye. But she had neither the time nor the opportunity to reassure him of her true intentions. No, manipulating these boors into abandoning their suit was taking all of her energy…and she was nearing exhaustion.

She had already managed to turn them against each other by courting them all simultaneously and then stepping back as they traded insults and threats while vying for her attention. She hid a smile behind her fan. Count Vitaly had already stormed away, cursing and muttering that she was not worth the trouble. And now the remaining two were at each other's throats.

Ekaterina eyed the squabbling men above her. Yes, it might take the better part of the day, but she could finagle her way out of this marriage business yet. All she had to do was make her suitors leave of their own volition. That would buy her enough time to escape her aunt's devious plans.

But Andrey…

She could no longer find him in her peripheral vision. She knew he must think her fickle or mad for shamelessly using her feminine wiles to court disaster. She was sure he did not understand what she was trying to do. She sighed inwardly and turned her attention back to outmanoeuvring her aunt.

In fact, Andrey wasn't even in the hall anymore. After seeing Ekaterina giggling at one of Boris's jokes and gasping in delight when Igor stroked her cheek, he'd found he could take no more. He'd marched out, heading straight for his workshop, which was abandoned for the day's festivities.

For the next few hours he lost himself in woodcarving. He started out by hacking aimlessly at a chunk of wood. By the time he had worked out most of his frustration, his shirt was soaked in sweat. He pulled the clinging material from his body and tossed it away. Then he began to chisel away at the wood with more purpose and less anger, letting the monotony of the work distract him.

So engrossed was he with his work that he almost missed the soft sound of a woman clearing her throat. He looked up, surprised.

'I thought I might find you here,' Ekaterina said softly as she stepped into his haven.

Andrey looked down, returning to his work.

'What are you doing here?' he asked gruffly.

'Don't be cross with me,' she said as she made her way over to his workbench. 'I only did what I had to.'

His answering laugh was a sharp, bitter bark.

'And did you choose a suitable husband?'

He waited for her reply, his eyes locked on to his wooden carving. But she said nothing, and the only sounds in the room were those of his chisel and hammer.

'Well?'

'Oh, Andrey.'

He paused midstroke. He felt her step up behind him and place one dainty hand on his shoulder.

'Well?' he asked again, his voice strained.

'Please look at me,' she said softly, stepping so close that he could feel her warmth against his back.

'I can't.'

'You don't understand,' she said, pressing up against him and smoothing her hands over his ribs.

'Then explain it to me.'

'I'm not marrying any of them.'

He paused and turned to face her.

'What?'

She looked up, her blue eyes wide and sincere.

'My aunt will be furious,' she continued. 'But none of those men will be my husband.'

'How is that possible?' Andrey asked with a frown.

She smiled.

'Because I chased them away. Igor managed to threaten the other two, and then I convinced Igor that I just wasn't worth the effort. He wasn't interested in marrying me once I let him believe that I don't stand to inherit much of anything from my father. Of course the fools had no idea that they'd been tricked.'

'So all that flirting…'

'A farce, Andrey.'

Andrey lowered his head, touching his forehead to

hers in relief. He'd underestimated her once again, and guilt flooded him.

'Did you think me so fickle?' she chided, clicking her tongue.

'I am a fool among fools,' Andrey admitted hoarsely.

She cupped his cheeks, her eyes meeting his earnestly. A sweet smile graced her lips.

'We were both cornered by my aunt,' she said, feathering kisses over the bridge of his nose. 'I had so very few choices. And there was no time to explain.'

He kissed her. It was a long, languorous kiss that was sweet with the slide of lips and tongue. Ekaterina pulled away first, and Andrey groaned.

'Andrey,' she breathed, her eyes searching his. 'My Andrey. I still don't know what will happen to us. My aunt will probably send me away, and I am not sure if I can save you from Siberia.'

She pressed closer to him, her fingers tangling in his hair. 'I will do my best, but…' She paused, her eyes welling with tears. 'But I'm not sure if we will be able to be together again.'

Andrey planted kisses over her eyes, his rough fingers drawing her close.

'Then let us make the most of the time we have left.'

His next kiss was hungry and demanding, as if he wanted to capture her and devour her whole. She responded with a low, throaty moan. When Ekaterina lifted her slim arms to twine them around his neck, her lips hot and wet against his, Andrey reached for the laces of her corset. With a few sharp tugs he pulled the bodice apart and let it drop to the floor in a bloom of dust. He spun her around suddenly, his hands sliding greedily over her bare skin.

Ekaterina let her head drop back, and Andrey laved her neck with his tongue. Her breaths came in quick, almost anguished pants as a delectable, unquenchable heat climbed her belly. Andrey grabbed at her skirt, his hands disappearing to smooth up her thighs.

'Andrey,' she begged, her breathing hitching in her throat.

Grunting, Andrey gently bent her over his workbench, his hands guiding hers into grabbing hold of the sculpture he'd just been working on. Hooking one arm around her waist, he pulled impatiently at his trousers. Then he pushed up her skirts and hiked them over her hips. Pressing his hot, throbbing member to her bottom, he leaned over her prone form and put his lips to her ear.

'Are you ready?' Andrey asked, his breath hot and ragged on the shell of her ear.

Ekaterina responded by grinding her hips against his and arching her back under his palm. Andrey gripped her hips with his hands and slowly pushed himself into her, his body shuddering with the exquisite sensation of her clenching around him. As he withdrew and thrust anew, Ekaterina's back arched and her fingers tightened around the carving. The sound of skin slapping against skin filled the dusty workshop, punctuated by their cries of pleasure.

For Andrey, it was a fantasy brought to life to have the woman of his dreams bent over his worktable, writhing beneath his pulsing rhythm and crying out his name in rapture. He planted a line of kisses down the line of her spine, grinning as she shivered. His hands moulded to her pert breasts and he rubbed her aching nipples with his callused thumbs.

Then, to his surprise, Ekaterina pulled away and his shaft bobbed free. Andrey growled in frustration, but Ekaterina simply turned around with a brazen smirk. With two deft tugs, her voluminous skirts slid down her slender hips to pool at the floor around her feet. Running the tip of her tongue across her bottom lip, she backed up and perched her bottom on the edge of Andrey's worktable. Arching one brow, and with a saucy tilt to her chin, she gracefully crossed one leg over her knee.

Andrey swallowed the lump in his throat as he grew impossibly harder. He leaned over her, planting his hands on either side of her hips.

'I think your legs are in the wrong position, Ekaterina,' he purred wickedly.

'Oh?' she teased playfully. 'And how do you think I *should* be sitting?'

'Let me show you.'

Andrey smoothed his hands up her shapely calves, hooking his fingers under her knees. With a sharp jerk, he pulled her legs apart and pressed his hips to her core.

'Oh,' she breathed, twisting her ankles around his waist.

'I will make you remember me,' he promised in low, determined tones.

Andrey grinned and leaned her back against the dusty table, sliding his open palm from her jaw to her breast. With a flash of teeth he surged forward, burying himself to the hilt. Ekaterina arched off the surface but Andrey pinned her hips down, relentlessly thrusting. He leaned over her, and she dug her fingers into his muscular shoulder blades. She inhaled the heady musk of his sweat, with the chalky scent of sawdust a pleasant undertone. She scraped her teeth over his neck, relishing the salt on his skin.

Then he angled his hips *just so* and her world exploded in white spots. For an endless moment there was nothing but sweat, skin and the rasp of their breathing. And then he gave a primal cry, filling her with a violent shudder.

Andrey buried his face in her bosom, panting and murmuring her name. She gathered him closer, her fingers tangling in his thick locks. They stayed locked in that embrace for as long as they could, each passing moment more precious than the one before. When finally they separated, they dressed slowly and reluctantly. They did not know what the evening would bring.

Right before they parted, Andrey gently pressed his lips to her knuckles. His eyes met hers.

'Until we meet again, my lady.'

Chapter Seven

Empress Anna was positively *seething*.

She paced the length of her royal chambers, muttering and casting glares at the two people standing in her reception area. There was the architect's apprentice, Andrey, who stood tall and broad-shouldered, his lips thin and his eyes grave. And then there was her niece, Ekaterina, with her fierce blue eyes and a defiant slant to her chin.

But appearances were deceiving. Andrey's palms were clammy and Ekaterina's stomach was turning somersaults. Neither knew what Empress Anna would do.

'Foolish girl,' the Empress bellowed as she turned on Ekaterina. 'You've toyed with my commands and turned my own subjects against me.'

'You misunderstand, Aunt,' Ekaterina replied, her voice cool. 'My suitors abandoned me.'

'Manipulative minx,' her aunt countered. 'You are delving into a game you can't hope to win.' Anna advanced on her, chest heaving in anger. 'Well, you can take your little aspirations back to the North, you ungrateful girl,' the Empress told her, teeth clacking together as she spoke. 'You are banished from my court, Ekaterina Romanova. Go back to your father. Tonight!'

Ekaterina resisted the urge to shrug. Such a sentence was hardly even a punishment. She'd never wanted to come to the Winter Court anyway. Now she was only worried for Andrey.

'And you,' the Empress said venomously, jabbing a finger in Andrey's direction. 'You should thank your lucky stars that your mentor has brought to my attention that the work on this palace would never be finished without you.'

Andrey's breath caught in his throat as he dared hope.

The Empress turned away, her hands clenching. She suddenly slammed her fist into a table and spun around, her cheeks aflame. Andrey felt his heart sink.

'I will give you a month to finish here, and then,' she hissed, enraged, 'you will be off to Siberia whether or not you are done. You will spend the rest of your life hauling goods under the whip, until your beautiful back is torn to ribbons and your jaw cracks under the strain. You will die my slave, Andrey Kvasov, this I promise you.'

Ekaterina's voice, clear and melodic, cut through the fog of his panic.

'I'm sorry, Aunt,' she said evenly, 'but that will not be possible.'

Both the Empress and Andrey turned to look at her, bewildered.

'Are you mad?' the Empress sputtered. 'Do you think you can command me?'

'No, Empress.'

Ekaterina steeled herself and straightened imperceptibly. She forced every ounce of her aristocratic upbringing into her next words.

'But you cannot send this architect to Siberia.'

Her aunt spat, her expression shocked and enraged. Ekaterina stared down her aunt, commanding and glacial. Andrey had never been so proud or so terrified.

'You. *You!*' the Empress stammered, for once at a loss for words.

Ekaterina took a breath and got ready to put her plan into motion. All the other pieces had fallen into place; now she just needed to trap her aunt.

'I am Ekaterina Romanova of the North,' she said, lifting her eyes proudly. 'And my father, the Baron Dimitri, has requested the services of the architect Andrey Kvasov in this letter.'

She held out a parchment, which her aunt snatched away. Her beady eyes scanned the scrawled words. Her face grew even redder, her cheeks puffing in aggravation.

'That scheming brother of mine,' she said through gritted teeth. 'How dare he?'

'How *dare* he?' Ekaterina sniffed delicately. 'When without his funds you would not be able to maintain this palace? We all know how much you rely on his money.'

Empress Anna looked as if she was about to explode. Both Andrey and Ekaterina fought to keep their ground. Shaking her finger at her niece, Empress Anna finally conceded defeat.

'You conniving little fox,' she spat. 'You are nothing but a thorn in my side. Get out.' She turned away in a huff. 'Both of you—out of my sight!'

They did not need any other encouragement. Without a moment's hesitation they marched from the royal suite, leaving the Empress to sulk by herself.

As soon as they were far enough, they both stopped and embraced in relief. Ekaterina grabbed Andrey's shirt and pulled him close.

'I must not linger,' she told him in a low voice. 'We have angered her enough, and who knows how she will retaliate if I stay but a moment too long?'

'Then go,' Andrey urged her, pressing a kiss to her

temple. 'But know that you and your father have surely saved my life.'

Her answering smile was gentle. She cupped his cheek and pressed a soft kiss on his lips.

'We will meet again,' she promised.

'Yes,' Andrey agreed. 'In a month I will come to you in the North.'

Ekaterina sighed and kissed him one last time.

'Stay out of her way. Stay safe.'

With that, she turned and hurried away, brushing away the tears that had collected at the corners of her eyes. Their farewell had been too brief, too rushed— but she knew that time was of the essence. She had to go, and she had to go now. Hopefully all would be well; *hopefully*.

'Ekaterina!'

She stopped and glanced over her shoulder at the sound of him calling her name. Her breath caught in her throat. His eyes were grave, but his smile was wicked and brave.

'I will build you as many secret passages as it pleases us to use.'

Ekaterina blew Andrey a cheeky kiss and winked, her heart swelling. Yes, they still had much to explore together…and she had many more games to play.

* * * * *

A SHOCKING PROPOSITION

Elizabeth Rolls

For Michelle Styles,
with grateful thanks for a wonderful
few days exploring Northumberland

Award-winning author **Elizabeth Rolls** lives in the Adelaide Hills of South Australia in an old stone farmhouse surrounded by apple, pear and cherry orchards, with her husband, two sons, three dogs and two cats. She also has four alpacas and three incredibly fat sheep, all gainfully employed as environmentally sustainable lawnmowers. The kids are convinced that writing is a perfectly normal profession, and she's working on her husband. Elizabeth has what most people would consider far too many books, and her tea and coffee habit is legendary. She enjoys reading, walking, cooking and her husband's gardening. Elizabeth loves to hear from readers and invites you to contact her via e-mail at books@elizabethrolls.com.

Chapter One

The dusty clock on the chimneypiece ticked inexorably as Madeleine Kirkby swallowed hard, gloved fingers tightened on her reticule. 'The court won't rule in my favour? You are quite, quite sure, sir?' If Mr Blakiston was correct, then a little mental arithmetic would allow her to calculate the exact seconds left for the clock to count down before she lost her home.

The old lawyer, in his dusty black, sighed. 'I am afraid not, Miss Maddy. You see, it is not considered wise to leave property, an *estate*, in the control of an unmarried woman. In your case, a young woman.'

'But I have been running the estate for *years*!' she said. 'Even before my brother died.' Fury lashed her. Stephen had left her to manage his inheritance while he disported himself in London. Yet *she* was considered unfit to own Haydon.

Mr Blakiston's mouth was grim, but he reached over the desk and touched her hand gently. 'I know, my dear, and I put all those arguments, but your grandfather's will was hard to argue against, and your cousin—well.'

It didn't need to be said. Edward, fifth Earl of Montfort, not content with his own much larger holdings, was determined to wrest Haydon from her hands. He and his father before him had bitterly resented that the third earl had dowered his daughter, Maddy's mother, with the old manor house and its estate.

'I suppose he'd have the judges in his pocket,' she said bitterly.

Mr Blakiston, his ears a little pink, said carefully, 'There was some talk that you are taking in women of…er…dubious reputation, and that, in short, there was some question as to your own…er…behaviour.' By the end of this Mr Blakiston's ears were glowing.

Outrage bubbled up. 'I took in a dairymaid that my cousin had ruined. Raped, in fact. She is fifteen! A child! And what of Edward's refusal to permit my marriage?'

As her nearest male relative, the moment Stephen had died Edward had petitioned the courts to name him her natural protector. He had no power over Haydon—Mr Blakiston was her trustee—but he had the power to block any marriage until she turned twenty-one.

The lawyer cleared his throat. 'As to that, apparently his lordship has made you an offer of marriage himself?'

Maddy clenched her fists at the hopeful note in her lawyer's voice. 'You think I should marry the sort of man who rapes the dairymaids? Yes, he did offer. I refused and he made it clear he would not consent to any other marriage for me! That if I did manage to get married without his consent he would have the marriage set aside. In fact, he has made it utterly impossible for me to fulfil the requirements of our grandfather's will.'

And not just by refusing his consent. He had smirched her reputation at every turn, making her a social outcast here in Newcastle. She doubted there was a gentleman the length and breadth of Britain who would have her to wife now. Certainly not one anywhere between the Tweed and the Tees. Not that she particularly wanted a husband, unless it helped her to save Haydon.

'I'm sorry, Miss Maddy,' said the lawyer quietly. 'But unless you mounted a challenge in Chancery, there is nothing you can do. His lordship takes possession of Haydon on the seventh of January.'

She didn't have the money to mount a case in Chancery, and her twenty-first birthday was not until Christmas Eve. Hardly sufficient time to find a husband before Epiphany in the best of circumstances. And now, with Christmas coming, she would have to tell her people that she had failed them. That she had lost.

'They would not give me until Lady Day?' she suggested. The end of March; that might be enough time....

Mr Blakiston shook his head. 'No, my dear. I did suggest that, but it was not looked upon favourably.'

Maddy's heart sank. Her home and her people were lost. She knew what Edward would do. Kick everyone out and demolish the manor for the dressed stone. All he wanted was extra acres for his sheep. He didn't care about the people who would lose their livelihoods, families broken apart, children who would end up in factories.

The office door opened and a clerk put his head in. 'His lordship is here, Mr Blakiston, sir. Should I ask him to wait?'

Maddy went cold. 'His lordship?' Surely—

Mr Blakiston smiled reassuringly. 'Lord Ashton Ravensfell, the duke's brother. He has some business with me. You are acquainted with him?'

'Yes.' Memory swept over her and her clenched fists relaxed. 'But I haven't seen Lord Ashton for years. Not since he bought his commission.' She had cried her eyes out when he had gone to war.

Mr Blakiston looked at the waiting clerk and a considering look came over his face. 'Thank you, Felton. Show his lordship straight in.'

Biting her lip, Maddy accepted that as a hint. She had probably wasted quite enough of the lawyer's time asking him to tilt at windmills for her. She rose. 'I'll bid you good day, sir. Thank you for—'

'No, no, Miss Maddy.' Hurriedly he rose and waved her back. 'There is no hurry. I am sure Lord Ashton will be happy to renew his acquaintance with you.'

She flushed, gathering her documents. 'No, I'd better go.' She'd been about fifteen when she had last seen Lord Ashton, and foolishly in love with him in the way that only a fifteen-year-old girl could be. She hoped devoutly that he'd never realised how her heart skipped at the sight of him and all the times she'd tried to imagine what it would be like if he suddenly swept her into his arms and declared his love. 'I doubt he would remember—'

'Lord Ashton, Mr Blakiston.' Felton the clerk was holding the door open.

Mr Blakiston went forward. 'Lord Ashton. I believe you are acquainted with Miss Kirkby?'

To her embarrassment, her heart leaped just as it always had at the sight of him. And then she froze as bleak grey eyes raked her and a frown creased his brow as he stared at her. And not as if he recalled her at all, let alone fondly.

Lord Ashton, brother to the fourth Duke of Thirlmere, was not quite as she remembered him. Oh, he was still tall, and with that head of fair hair and sea-grey eyes that proclaimed his Viking forebears. And years of fighting Napoleon's forces in the Peninsula had left him with all

his limbs and no obvious scars. But there was an inde-
finable difference in him that had little to do with age
and everything, she thought, to do with experience.

'Miss—?' The frown lightened a little, and his mouth
achieved something that might have been a smile, but
didn't warm his eyes. 'Of course. Miss Kirkby.'

He held out his hand, bowed over hers, exquisitely polite. Heat and cold swept Maddy as his gloved hand held
hers, and she managed to get out a polite reply even as
her heart still thumped and her pulse skittered.

'God help me! It's you again. Nuisancy brat!'

She remembered him calling her that. Then he'd smile
at her and tell her to tie her pony up and keep her mis-
begotten dog out of the way.

Those pleasantries aside, Ash Ravensfell had always
had a friendly smile for her. Even when he'd been grum-
bling at her and threatening her pony and herself with
a gruesome death if either of them stood on any of the
Roman antiquities he had found near her home. Papa had
never minded Lord Ash digging near the Wall.

'No time for that nonsense. He's welcome to it all.'

Sometimes he'd let her uncover something he'd found.
A coin, a piece of pottery, once a little bronze horse, its
head upflung. He'd explained what the discovery was.
What he thought it meant. Then the grey eyes had held
laughter. Now they held ghosts, as if he'd found things

he'd rather forget, and he mouthed stiff, polite greetings as if to a stranger.

He's a duke's brother. You're far beneath him in the scheme of things.

Only, the Ash Ravensfell she remembered hadn't seemed above her at all. He'd been a friend.

She got a smile onto her face and made her excuses in a stultifyingly proper voice that even her great-aunt Maria couldn't have faulted, and left.

Mr Blakiston saw her out, ignoring her protests. 'Not at all, my dear. I am only sorry I cannot help you any further. I had better get back to his lordship. Rather an awkward commission. He wishes to buy a property of his own.'

Something about the way his eyes held hers alerted her. 'A property?'

'Yes.' The lawyer shook his head. 'Not too large, you know. And near the old Roman Wall. His lordship is very interested in antiquities.'

'Yes,' she said slowly. 'I remember that.'

Mr Blakiston patted her hand. 'Sadly, I have not the particulars of a single property like that to interest him yet. One or two that might do at a pinch, but I fear he will be disappointed. They are either too far away or too large. Well, I had best go and break the bad news. Goodbye, my dear.' And he squeezed her hand.

* * *

Maddy made her way slowly back towards the Three Shepherds Inn, where she had stabled her horse and gig, stopping off on the way to buy tea, her mind spinning.

Her mind continued to spin as she left the tea merchant's shop. Mr Blakiston was usually the soul of discretion. She didn't think he had ever, in all her dealings with him, had another client ushered in while the previous client was still with him. Of course, that might be because he no longer considered her a client. In just over a month she wouldn't be. But then, why had he confided Lord Ashton's business to her? He had a reputation for being close-mouthed. He *never* gossiped about clients... did he? Surely he hadn't been giving her a hint?

But what if he had? Was there a way to save her home? Her people?

She knew Ash Ravensfell. Or she'd thought she did. For all his familiarity, the man in Blakiston's chambers just now had been a stranger.

But if he wants a property near the Wall... What if...?

She was nearly at the inn, and her steps slowed. Christmas was so close. She would have to tell her people that there was no hope, unless—

'Well, well, well. It's my little cousin. And did Blakiston break the news gently?'

Maddy looked up. Edward, Earl of Montfort, stood there by the archway leading into the stable yard of the

Three Shepherds. Tall, dark, handsome… His aristocratic features had been known to make maidens sigh.

Maddy wanted to spit on them.

'Or were you looking for lodgings here?' Edward's smile oozed gloating self-satisfaction. 'Haydon will be mine on the seventh of January. You'd better start packing.'

It was his smug assurance that did it.

'You're counting chickens rather early, aren't you, Edward?' she said sweetly. 'You really ought to wait until they're hatched. And even then a fox might take them if the run isn't secure.'

He laughed at her. 'You're a fool, Madeleine. If you'd had any sense you'd have accepted my offer of marriage.'

'And spent the rest of my life protecting the dairymaids?' she shot back.

Determined to wrest Haydon back, he'd offered marriage only because he wanted everyone to know that he hadn't simply kicked her out. That, and it would have made taking Haydon easier. Marrying him would have saved her, but not Haydon. He'd made it very clear that he intended to demolish the old manor for the building stone and the section of the Roman Wall that marched across the estate.

He roared with laughter. 'Did that rankle? Were you expecting me to save myself for you?'

'You mean, did I expect you to behave like a gentleman, Edward?' she suggested. 'Good God, no.'

That wiped the smirk from his face, and he came towards her. She held her ground, telling herself there was little enough he could do here in a busy yard.

'Everything all right, Miss Maddy?' called a stableman crossing the yard with a horse.

Edward swung towards him. 'You'll mind your own business, fellow, if you know what's good for you!'

The man hesitated, and Edward gripped her arm, ignoring him. 'We'll have a little talk in private, cousin,' he said in a low, hard voice. 'And if you put up a fuss and one of these gapeseeds is fool enough to interfere, I'll see that he loses his position!'

'A great many witnesses, Edward,' she said, digging in her heels. 'Talk here.' The last thing she wanted was Jed the stableman interfering on her behalf and getting into trouble for it.

She bit back a cry as Edward's grip tightened, and, exerting his strength, he began to drag her to the side entrance. Fear rose, a choking ball in her throat, and with her free hand she struck at his face, mentally cursing her gloves that made scratching impossible.

He jerked his head back to avoid the blow. *'Bitch!'*

'Miss Kirkby!'

Booted footsteps sounded on the cobbles behind them, and with a muttered curse Edward released her arm.

She turned, resisting the urge to rub her arm, and her heart, already pounding, skipped a beat. Lord Ashton stood there, grey eyes narrowed to blazing slits as he confronted Edward. Several stablemen had appeared and ranged themselves nearby, including Jed.

'I suggest that you leave the lady alone, Montfort,' Lord Ashton said quietly.

'Who the he—?' Edward broke off, staring. 'Good Lord! It's Ravensfell, isn't it? I saw your brother the other day. He mentioned you were back.' He approached Lord Ashton, holding out his hand. 'Travelling on the Continent, weren't you?'

Lord Ashton merely stared down his nose, and Edward took an involuntary step back.

He recovered, waving his hand at Maddy with a conspiratorial smile for Lord Ashton. 'Just a little cousinly spat. You know how it is with women. I'm forever telling her she ought not to jaunter about alone, but will the silly chit listen to me?'

Lord Ashton turned to Maddy. 'Miss Kirkby?'

She said simply, 'My cousin desired some private conversation. Since I have nothing to say to him, and no desire to hear anything he may wish to say that cannot be said in public, I declined.' And she deliberately rubbed her arm where Edward had gripped it.

Lord Ashton's eyes seemed to settle there and narrow to dangerous slits.

'That would appear to settle it, Montfort,' he said in a voice that might have been chipped off an iceberg. 'The lady refused. In my book that always ends the matter.' A hint of scorn laced his tones.

Edward scowled. 'See here, Ravensfell, you've no call to interfere. If my cousin and I—'

'Leave me out of it, Edward,' said Maddy. 'I've no desire to speak to you. Unless, of course, you wish to discuss a settlement for Cally Whitfield. She's expecting your child in a few months.'

Edward's mouth opened and closed, and Lord Ashton's chill grey eyes widened slightly.

Maddy watched Edward contemptuously. 'No, cousin? I thought not.'

She turned away from him.

'Thank you, Lord Ashton.'

He inclined his head. 'Not at all. Are you returning home now?'

Maddy's mind whirled. She'd intended to have Bunty put to and drive straight home. It was after midday. If she didn't hurry, darkness would catch her before she reached Haydon. She cast a glance at the sky. It was bright and clear, and last night's sunset had been brilliant. *Red sky at night, shepherd's delight.* And there would be a moon if she needed it...

'Not quite at once, sir.' Her heart pounded at the sheer impropriety of what she was about to do, but she had no further doubts. 'There is one piece of business I need to conclude.'

He nodded. 'I see.' He glanced at Edward. 'I cannot see that you have anything further to do here, Montfort. Unless your horses are here? No? Then, good day.'

Lord Ashton didn't move. There was nothing overtly threatening in his appearance or voice. But something about the cold grey eyes and his stance radiated a warning, and Maddy stared as her cousin, his eyes hard, turned on his heel and stalked out of the yard.

One of the lingering stablemen muttered, 'An' a good riddance, too.'

Five minutes later Maddy was ensconced in a private parlour with pen and paper provided by a very curious landlord. Her stomach still churned at what she was doing, not to mention the confrontation with Edward, and she fought to keep her hand steady enough to produce the perfect copperplate her governess had drilled into her.

It took her half an hour and several sheets of paper to say what she needed to say. Resisting the urge to read it over yet again, Maddy folded up her letter, wrote the direction upon it and affixed the wafer. She had made it as businesslike as she could.

Nothing ventured, nothing won. And she had absolutely nothing to lose. She sent word for her horse to be put to, and sallied back out to the yard.

To find that Lord Ashton was waiting for her by the gig, his horse saddled.

'You're escorting me home?' Maddy Kirkby stared at him, her face crimson.

Ash resisted the temptation to touch a finger lightly to her cheek and find out if the blush really was scorching. Or if her skin was as silken as it looked. Instead, he held out his hand to assist her up into the gig.

'Yes.'

Her hand was gloved. That ought to be safe enough, even if the shock of seeing her again in Blakiston's office had reduced him to inanities.

If anything her blush deepened. 'There's no need for that!'

He said nothing, just raised one eyebrow. Judging by her expression, that still annoyed her as much as ever.

'You're going to insist, aren't you?' she said, sounding as though her back teeth were clenched together.

He nodded. 'I am.'

Silence sizzled between them for a moment. There was something about her. About the tilt of her chin and the narrowing of her green eyes that told him she was as stubborn a woman as she had been a child. He'd never realised how attractive stubborn could be.

With a snort, she accepted his hand and stepped into the gig. 'Thank you,' she said. 'Even though it isn't necessary!'

'Thank *you*,' he said, fighting a wholly unexpected urge to grin. Stubborn, but definitely not stupid.

'For what?' she asked in a suspicious voice.

'For not wasting time and breath with an argument you weren't going to win,' he said, watching as she tucked a fur rug about her legs. He'd be damned if he'd let her drive home alone. He swung into the saddle and followed her out of the yard.

There was too much traffic in the town to ride beside the gig, let alone converse, but once they were clear and out on the Corbridge road he brought his mare up alongside. By then he'd noted that she was an excellent whip. Sure and steady, keeping her little mare well up to her bit. He wouldn't have minded being driven by her. He also knew that his decision to escort Maddy home had been well founded.

'Look, for what it's worth, Maddy—Miss Kirkby, I mean—I have no doubt that you are perfectly capable of looking after yourself.'

She let out a breath. 'You always used to call me Maddy. When you weren't calling me a nuisancy brat.'

'You aren't a brat anymore,' he pointed out. God help him, she was a woman. He knew that happened—of course he did—but... He swallowed, trying not to think about the stray tawny curl that flirted beside her temple. 'Are you saying I may still call you Maddy?'

Something in him tensed. *Maddy.* It sounded so damn intimate. Last time he'd seen her she'd been about fifteen with a mass of springy, curly hair tied back in a ponytail he'd occasionally pulled. Now he ached to twist that stray curl around his finger, brush it back.

'Yes. If you wish.'

She was an old friend, he reminded himself. That was all.

'Then you had better drop the Lord Ashton rubbish,' he said. 'It's still Ash.' That was how it should be between friends.

'You thought Edward might waylay me, didn't you?' she said.

And she was still as quick of thought as she had ever been.

For a moment Ash hesitated. 'He thought about it,' he said. 'He changed his mind when he saw I was with you.'

'What?'

He'd thought she hadn't noticed Montfort lurking near the edge of the town as they drove out. She'd needed all her concentration on her driving to clear a dray.

She muttered something under her breath, and paled.

She feared Montfort?

'Who is Cally?' he asked.

Her mouth tightened. 'A dairymaid. Who didn't have anyone around to defend her when she said no.'

'I see.' And he did. The world was full of Callys. And unfortunately full of Montforts. Sadly, not so full of women like Maddy who would stand by the poor girl. 'You've taken her in?'

A short nod.

'What did your brother say to that?'

Her shocked expression as she turned to him gave the clue.

'You didn't know? But that's why Edward—' she broke off. 'I'm sorry. Stephen died six months ago.'

That's why Edward... What? He didn't like to ask since she hadn't volunteered the information. 'I'm very sorry,' he said instead. 'My condolences.' A thought occurred to him. 'Er...am I still escorting you to Haydon?'

A queer expression flashed across her face, gone in an instant. 'Yes. I still live there. Mr Blakiston said that you are still interested in Roman antiquities.'

A change of subject if ever he'd heard one, but he accepted it. He felt relaxed in a way he hadn't for a long time. Somehow, talking to Maddy about the Wall, his summer plans for excavating one of the forts he knew of, took him back to summer days before he'd gone to war. When Maddy had still worn her hair down, albeit tied back against the eternal wind that swept the fells. And those bright green eyes had been nearly as quick to spot a half-buried potsherd as his own. He still had the little horse he'd found one day when she was there. A collector in Rome had wanted to buy it, but he hadn't been able to bring himself to part with it.

They were still talking when they reached the turn-off up to the village of Haydon.

Maddy halted the gig there, sheltered from the wind's bite in the lee of the hedge. 'I would invite you up, but it's getting late. If you don't turn back now—' She glanced up at the sky.

She was right, but the regret that shot through him was a complete surprise. He wanted to spend more time with her. Find out why she'd used that odd phrase—*I still live there*. His jaw tensed—and find out why she feared Montfort. Did he own Haydon now? Somehow Ash didn't much like the thought of that.

'Thank you for accompanying me home,' she said, holding out her hand. 'Not just because of Edward, but—' She stopped, her face flooding scarlet.

Because she had enjoyed his company? As much as he had enjoyed hers?

'I'll see you in the summer, if not before,' he said. And realised that he definitely didn't want to wait that long. 'You won't mind my digging on Haydon land again?'

A queer expression crossed her face. It almost, he thought, looked like guilt. 'N-No. But we'll need to discuss it.' She held out her hand.

'Of course,' he said.

He leaned over to take her gloved hand, meaning only to say goodbye. For an instant her fingers clung and their eyes met. Slowly, giving her every chance to pull back, he turned her hand over, palm up. There, between glove and sleeve, was the merest strip of pale, tempting skin. Heat a swift rhythm in his blood, he raised her wrist to his mouth and brushed his lips over the place. Lord, she was soft. Tissue soft, silk soft. His lips lingered, and he breathed in a new world. Breathed in leather, wool, lavender and, beneath all that, the underlying fragrance of warm, sweet woman.

For a fleeting instant there was madness, his fingers tightening involuntarily. And then his brain re-engaged, banishing insanity. Reluctantly, rebellion pounding in every pulse of his blood, he obeyed its dictates and straightened, releasing her.

In the real world the earth and sky were, to his surprise, still in their proper relation, the one to the other. Somewhere a rook cawed lazily, a dog barked and the wind whipped at them. Nothing had changed. Except Maddy Kirkby was staring at him, green eyes wide, and her lips, which had at some time in the past several years become shockingly lush, slightly parted.

'You had better go,' he said, rather more roughly than he liked. But God help him if she continued to look at him like that. Her parted lips were giving him ideas.

Ideas a gentleman who had taken self-righteous exception to another man's behaviour was a complete hypocrite to be entertaining.

Her mouth closed and colour flared in her cheeks, her chin lifting as she gathered up the ribbons and set her mare in motion. Her eyes flashed a challenge. 'I am not a toy for your amusement, Ash Ravensfell,' she said quietly.

The mare's breath huffed out on the cold air and they were trotting away up the lane.

He watched even after the gig had rounded the first bend, still able to see Maddy, spear straight, until she crested the rise and was gone.

Chapter Two

The horse—he was fairly sure it was his, although it was not in the least familiar—picked its steady way along a ridge. Despite the drifting mists, he knew precisely where he was—on Haydon land near Hadrian's Wall. Somewhere in the whiteness ahead he could hear the sound of stone scraping, tools being used on the Wall. He tried to push the horse faster, knowing that some vandal was dismantling part of the Wall for building stone, but the horse ignored his efforts. Wind swirled down out of the north, and on the Wall just ahead of him a figure became visible...a woman in a dark cloak, tawny hair tumbling about her shoulders in wild disarray and witch-green eyes. Waiting for him. She held out her hand, either beseeching his aid or offering her own. He tried to speak, but the Wall trembled and fell, and she was gone with it into the mist....

Ash woke to the sound of his curtains being drawn back and lay quietly. A better dream than most he'd had in the past eighteen months. At least he thought it was. Already it was fading.... Had he really dreamed that Maddy Kirkby had been standing on Hadrian's Wall, begging him for help? Or had she been going to help him?

Ash looked uninterestedly at the solitary unopened letter beside his breakfast plate and addressed himself half-heartedly to the very excellent ham and eggs on his plate. Opposite him his much elder half-brother, Gerald, Duke of Thirlmere, was going through his personal correspondence while munching toast and marmalade. Occasionally the ducal brows rose. Twice he snorted out a laugh and read something aloud to his duchess, Helen.

The duchess, glancing up from her own letters, smiled affectionately at her husband over the rim of her teacup. Both duke and duchess cast furtive glances at Ash.

He tried very hard not to notice and even harder not to grit his teeth. He knew they loved him, but he did wish they would stop worrying about him. But how did you explain to your brother, who was more like a father to you and had never been anywhere near a battlefield in his life, and his even more sheltered wife, that there was nothing wrong? Nothing that a complete loss of memory wouldn't fix.

At least he was sleeping better, and the dreams—dreams that had woken him screaming, and in a cold sweat of fear—weren't as frequent. In fact, he hadn't had one for a couple of months. Although he couldn't say that he entirely liked the turn his dreams had taken last night. *If* he had dreamed about Maddy Kirkby. He wasn't too sure now. Perhaps he had. He'd certainly spent enough time on the journey home yesterday thinking about her. Wondering if the rest of that milky pale skin was as sweet and silken as her wrist. Or the wide, lush mouth was as passionate as his imagination wanted it to be.

Hell's teeth! What was worse? Suffering nightmares, or indulging in erotic fantasies about a respectable young lady he hadn't seen since she was fifteen?

Of course, girls grew up, and the discomfort of his saddle yesterday had attested to the fact that Maddy had definitely grown up. He would see more of her in the summer if he excavated the fort on her land, so he'd better get over it.

Gerald, having finished with his letters, removed his eyeglasses and smeared a vast amount of marmalade on another piece of toast. Helen was gazing thoughtfully at the teapot, clearly considering another cup, and then she gave Ash another worried glance.

It had occurred to Ash in the past that if he just joined

in with whatever passed for normal at any given time, his brother and sister-in-law seemed to worry less. In that spirit he picked up the letter beside his plate and broke the wafer. Accustomed to noticing everything about him, because his life and those of his men might depend on detail, he registered the fact that the wafer had been affixed with a plain seal and the paper was of rather poor quality. On the other hand, the writing was that of an educated...woman, at a guess.

His gaze flicked to the signature—M. Kirkby—and his pulse skipped a beat. He quelled it, and noted the address—Three Shepherds Inn, Newcastle—which explained the plain seal and cheap paper. It also explained what she'd been doing yesterday while he waited for her. But why the devil hadn't she just told him whatever it was on the way out to Haydon?

He began to skim the letter and then, wondering if perhaps he was still asleep and dreaming, went back and started reading again. Slowly. When he'd finished, and was convinced he was actually awake, he read the letter again. Just in case he had missed something. He hadn't. It said precisely what he'd thought it said, and it certainly made sense that she hadn't quite liked to broach this subject face-to-face.

'Interesting letter, then, Ash?' said Gerald.

That was one way of putting it.... Ash handed the letter over. 'You tell me.'

Gerald stared at him, put his eyeglasses back on and glanced at the letter. 'Madeleine Kirkby? What's she doing writing to you?' He began to read. '"A business proposition to put to you...Grandfather's will—" Heard something about that. Rather an awkward business with Montfort being so determined to take the estate back, very poor showing on his part, if you ask me...' He glanced up, frowning. 'You didn't say that you'd seen her at old Blakiston's yesterday. Or that you'd had a run-in with Montfort. Fellow's a blister. A complete wart.'

Ash said nothing and Gerald fell silent again as he read on.

'Good God!' He looked up, removed his eyeglasses and stared at Ash.

Ash refilled his own coffee cup and leaned over to top up Gerald's for good measure. 'That's what I thought.'

'About what?' demanded the duchess.

Gerald put the letter down, took a sizeable swig of coffee. 'It's a proposal.'

'Yes, dear.' Helen adopted the sort of patient tone that a wife of twenty-five years who wanted to stay sane had to perfect. 'You mentioned a business proposal. What sort of business does Miss Kirkby have with Ash?'

'Marriage,' said Ash.

'I don't quite see what's bothering you about it,' Gerald said placidly as they rode.

The day was surprisingly clear, a miracle in early December. Gerald had said the weather would close in later and Ash agreed. But right now a pale sun filtered down, brightening the bleak fells with their dusting of snow.

'What?' Ash wasn't entirely sure he'd heard correctly. Gerald had asked if he planned to accept Miss Kirkby's offer and he'd answered that it probably wasn't a good idea.

Apparently Gerald didn't agree any more than his own unruly body had. The moment he had read Maddy's marriage proposal his body had proclaimed it an excellent idea.

Ash was having a hard enough time ignoring his baser instincts and listening to the dictates of honour, which said that he shouldn't take advantage of Maddy's situation, without Gerald's idiocy.

'I'm not fit to marry anyone!' he snapped.

The idea of waking up from a nightmare screaming, in bed with Maddy...no. Except Montfort was going to take her home, kick her out... He liked that idea even less. Edward Montfort needed a thrashing at the very least. He'd thought so yesterday. His hands tightened to fists on the reins and his mare tossed her head in annoyance.

'Why the hell not?' demanded Gerald. 'You're well enough off as these things go. Are you dishonest? The sort of blister who'd beat his wife?' He frowned at Ash's fidgeting mare. 'What's bothering Phaedre?'

'Of course not,' said Ash, easing his hands. The mare settled at once, and he met Gerald's calm gaze. Better to have the truth between them. 'For God's sake, Gerald! What woman wants a coward to husband?'

For a moment they rode on in silence, their horses' hooves ringing on the iron-hard ground.

'Ran away in the teeth of battle, did you?' asked Gerald at last.

'What?' Ash stared. 'No, of course not. But—'

'Oh. You hid in your tent and didn't even go out to fight?' Gerald nodded. 'See what you mean. Very bad form, that.'

'Don't be a bloody idiot!'

'That would be *you*,' said Gerald. 'And I'll thank you to stop insulting my brother, whoever you are. If you think a few bad dreams make you a coward, you *are* an idiot.'

'You don't—can't—understand,' said Ash. He'd been unable to hide the dreams from Gerald, but this was the first time the topic had been mentioned openly.

Gerald nodded. 'No. Not fully. You know, when I started learning to ride I had an accident. Only about four, but something spooked the pony and she bolted. Full-scale bolt. I hung on, absolutely terrified, as long as possible—'

'You were a child!' said Ash. 'That doesn't make you a coward!'

'I fell off in the end,' said Gerald, as if his brother hadn't spoken. 'Soft landing. Nothing broken. And they put me right back on, so I rode home. But that night I had nightmares and the next time I was taken out for a lesson I wouldn't get on. Screamed the place down. Wasn't so much the fall itself, but the bolt, I think—the *fear* of falling. Took weeks before I'd get on again. But I did get on in the end.'

'You were a child,' repeated Ash.

'I was,' agreed Gerald. 'And you weren't much more than a boy when you went out to the Peninsula and—'

'I was twenty-five!'

'That's what I said—a boy,' said Gerald, from the vantage point of the twilight side of fifty. 'And you saw God knows what, but I never heard you bottomed out or failed in your duty in any way. And you finished up at Waterloo.' He snorted. 'If you'd told me you hadn't been frightened I'd think you a damn fool.' He considered. 'Or a liar.'

There was nothing to say to that, and eventually Gerald spoke again, his voice slightly thicker.

'Thirty thousand men dead. I've often thought it must have been something like hell. And I can tell you it was hell waiting to know if you were one of those thirty thousand.'

It had been worse than hell, because the carnage had not distinguished between good and evil.... But perhaps Gerald did understand after all.... Who would have thought it? Kind, stolid, dependable Gerald, stuffed with duty to the backbone.

'The thing is,' said Gerald, 'we hang on for as long as we have to, even when we're terrified, but sometimes, man or boy, it takes time to...well, not to forget, you don't do that, but learn to see the memory from a distance or something.'

Was that what he needed to do?

Ash changed the subject. 'And you think I should marry Maddy Kirkby? I hardly know the girl!'

Which begged the question of that shattering *awareness* of her in Blakiston's office yesterday. And certainly didn't solve the problem of sharing a bed with a woman when you might wake up screaming.

Gerald snorted. 'Well, that's never been considered an impediment to marriage. If you think about it, it's no more odd than if her father or brother, were they alive, had approached me about an alliance between the pair of you. All Miss Kirkby has done is be rather more direct than is usual. Look at the facts, Ash. You've been offered exactly what you want—a property right on that blessed Wall of yours. If it comes with a wife attached, where's the problem? You seem to know her well enough to call her Maddy.'

He shot Ash a shrewd look.

'And for some reason you didn't see fit to mention to me that you'd seen her yesterday, let alone had some sort of run-in with Montfort over her.'

'I'd be marrying her for her money!' And her stretch of Wall, of course. He shoved aside the thought of Montfort. He'd settle with him soon enough.

Gerald shrugged. 'Happens all the time. And it was her idea. Look at it this way—if you don't marry her she'll be out on her ear and won't have any money.'

There was that. And there was also the shocking attraction he'd felt yesterday. He'd wanted to see her again, and here she was offering to marry him.

A business proposal. That's what she's offering.

'Seems to me,' said Gerald, 'that you'd be helping each other. You need something to do with your life. She needs to keep her home.'

Ash took in a deep breath. 'I'll have to see her again.'

Gerald nodded. 'Need to discuss the marriage settlements, for one thing. And while it's perfectly understandable that she proposed in a letter, the least you can do is accept in person.'

Chapter Three

It was mid-morning when Ash's mare clattered over the stone bridge into Haydon village, the river tumbling beneath. He'd spent the night in Newcastle after seeing Blakiston, who had seemed quite unsurprised by the visit, or the tentative instructions he'd been given.

'Certainly, my lord. A very sensible solution for both of you, if I may say so.'

Ash wasn't sure what sort of answer he'd returned. His head ached and his eyes and temper were scratchy from a poor night's sleep. Not the usual battle dreams, though, but dreams of Maddy again, this time soft and willing in his arms....

He shoved the images out of his head, trotting Phaedre through the little village clustered by the bridge. It hadn't changed since last he'd seen it. Grey stone houses huddled together along the narrow street, smoke drifting from their chimneys. The church, with its squat tower, nestled beside the rectory, and at the far end of the street, just before the road rose steeply towards Haydon itself, stood the Bowman's Arms.

It had stood there in one form or another for centuries. Ash knew it well, having often stayed there when he came down to this part of the county looking for Roman remains. He wondered if old Runcorn the landlord was still there, but rode past. Maybe he'd stop on the way back to Newcastle if he had time.

It had snowed lightly the night before and a thin drift of white lay over everything. Phaedre's breath steamed in the chilly air as she breasted the rise out of the village.

Higher and higher they climbed as the road curved round. As he recalled, Haydon was only a mile or so out of the village, perched on a steep drop above a bend in the river. He couldn't possibly get lost, because this road between the bare hedges led only to Haydon. He'd never been up to the castle in winter before, and even in summer it could be bleak. Now, even with his pounding head, his heart leaped at the bite of the wind and the threat of snow in the air.

At last the buildings came into view. Haydon Castle… Ash reined the mare in, looking. Compared to Gerald's pile, calling Haydon a castle was slightly overstating the case. It was more of a fortified manor, not really a castle at all. Still, it had an outer bailey, a courtyard that one might designate an inner bailey and a curtain wall. Once it had even had a portcullis, although he very much doubted it had ever kept any seriously pillage-minded Scots out. In these more peaceful times buildings had been erected outside the old fortifications. A barn, a cow byre larger than the one within the walls, several cottages. It was its own little world up here.

He nudged Phaedre and rode on, approaching the main gate. It stood wide open, but as he rode into the old outer bailey a fusillade of barking broke out and a very large black-and-white crossbred hound he remembered only too well charged through the gate that led to the inner bailey.

He drew rein and Phaedre halted, shifting restlessly as the dog stopped several yards away, still barking, hackles raised. Peaceful times, but Haydon retained some defences. Ash spoke soothingly to the mare and she settled, although wary of the barking dog.

'Ketch!' He spoke firmly, and at the sound of his name the dog wagged its tail but continued barking. 'Enough, Ketch. Sit.' That was how Maddy had always told the dog to stop barking.

Ketch sat, ears pricked.

A middle-aged man came through the gate, his eyes

narrowing suspiciously as he saw Ash. He cast a surprised glance at the dog.

'Aye? You lookin' for someone?'

Ketch's furious barking alerted Maddy, and she set down her pen. The dog only barked at strangers and people he disliked. Strangers rarely came here, even in summer, and the person Ketch disliked most was Edward. She gritted her teeth. If Edward thought to stalk through Haydon and make claims on belongings he had no right to, then he had another think coming.

She rose, set her papers aside neatly and went to stand by the fire. It was warmer there, and she'd be that much closer to a poker if Ketch and Brady, her steward, were unable to persuade him to go away. The barking had stopped, but she could hear the clop of hooves in the courtyard below. A visitor, then.... She waited.

The outer door to the great hall opened, admitting a blast of cold air and the man she had persuaded herself she was not going to see or even hear from, unless it was a curt 'no, thank you'—Ash Ravensfell.

Her jaw dropped as disbelief hit her like a pile of collapsing masonry. He walked in, saw her and at once removed his hat. Brady came in behind him, flanked by Ketch, who rushed forward and ranged himself beside her, tail whirling.

Aren't I clever, Mistress? See what I brought you!

Brady doffed his hat. 'Lord Ashton to see you, Miss Maddy.'

She said nothing. *Could* say nothing for the shock reverberating through her. Automatically she scratched Ketch's ears. He had come. Against all expectation, all likelihood, Ash Ravensfell had answered her letter. In person. What on earth was she going to do with him?

Brady frowned, casting a suspicious glance at Ash. 'Says you wrote to him?'

Maddy located her tongue and wits. 'Yes. Yes, I did write.' *Damn it!* She could scarcely breathe, let alone think or speak, with Ash watching her so closely. Her mind kept skittering back to the touch of his lips on her wrist. She managed a deep breath. At all costs she had to hide the effect he had on her. A business arrangement; that was all she had offered.

Perhaps he had come to refuse?

Ash spoke. 'I thought it less awkward to answer your letter in person rather than in a letter.'

Dear Miss Kirkby—Thank you for your kind offer, but I have other plans for my life.

Nothing awkward about that. Did he mean—? Was he actually considering her offer?

She pulled herself together. 'Thank you, my lord.'

His brows rose and she remembered the sound of her name on his lips. 'Er…thank you, Brady. If you go out by the kitchen you might ask Bets to bring up a pot of tea?' She looked at Ash. 'Or coffee?' He looked tired, she realised, as though he'd slept badly. Dark shadows wreathed his eyes, and his mouth looked grim. As though he had as many worries nipping at his heels as she did.

'Tea will be fine,' he said.

As they struggled through the niceties of him removing gloves, great coat and muffler and drawing near the fire, along with Maddy's stilted remarks about the weather and it being a long ride from his home, Ash wondered if she might be regretting her letter. The dog remained with them, close by Maddy's side. Ketch had not so much as growled at him again, but Ash knew that at the least threat to Maddy the dog would be in front of her, ready to defend. He'd once seen the dog take down a tramp who had threatened her.

He waited until an elderly woman appeared with a tea tray, along with a suspicious glare for him. She set the tray at one end of the huge refectory table, where it looked as though Maddy had been attending to some business, and left them.

'Will you be seated, sir?'

At the polite invitation, he said simply, 'You called me Ash the other day. Are we back to "sir" and "Miss Kirkby"?'

She flushed. 'I wasn't expecting you.'

'After that letter?' He snorted as he sat down. 'Curiosity, if nothing else, would have got me here.'

He watched her as she poured the tea, handed him a cup and a piece of shortbread. Her tawny hair was pinned up simply, as though she'd had no time for more, and the shadows he'd seen beneath her eyes the other day had deepened. Now he knew what had put them there, knew he could lift the weight of care from her slender shoulders.

He sipped his tea. 'Why me, Maddy?' His conversation with Blakiston had been illuminating, but he wanted to know why she would take this risk. Because it *was* a risk for her. She knew so little about him, and marriage could potentially hand him complete control of her lands and person. Why had she chosen to trust him?

Her cup rattled in its saucer as she set it down. 'Why? Because it's that or lose Haydon.'

'There were other fellows, Maddy. Men you knew better, who were prepared to brave Montfort's bluster and marry you. You refused them all.'

She bit her lip. 'They didn't actually want Haydon. Just the price of its sale, or the acres and the money they could get for letting the house, or even demolishing it for the stone. The Wall, too.'

His gut twisted, and as if she knew she looked up and met his gaze. 'Nor would it have saved my household. They would all have lost their positions, their homes.'

He nodded slowly. Blakiston had already told him this. She could have saved herself by marriage, but for her it was all or nothing. He knew from Blakiston that she ran Haydon efficiently. It wasn't a massive holding, but it was productive. She was managing perfectly well by herself. She didn't really need a husband; she just needed to save her home from Montfort.

And for himself? It would be the chance he wanted to excavate a stretch of the Wall uninterrupted. See if he was right about there being a fort on the northeast corner of Haydon land near the river.

And there was Madeleine Kirkby herself. The sort of woman who had chosen to stand with her people rather than save herself. The sort of woman who could haunt a man's dreams....

He glanced around as they drank their tea. The great hall looked much as he remembered it. Once, he thought, the walls would have been covered in tapestries, bright and glowing in the firelight. Instead, someone in the past century or so had added panelling in a rich, gleaming oak. Worn Turkish carpets were scattered here and there on the wide-planked floor. There were no paintings, but a pair of crossed swords beside the fireplace.

He gestured to them. 'Why not above the fireplace?'

She raised her brows. 'Harder to get at in a hurry.'

Wry amusement made him smile. 'Do you think the Scots are going to come marauding again?'

She laughed. 'No. But they've always been there.'

Tradition, then. He could respect that. 'Will you show me around?' he asked. 'I don't think I've ever been past this hall.'

She frowned. 'Why?'

He shrugged. 'If you expect me to invest, I need to see what you're offering.' *Apart from yourself.* He left that unsaid, and wished he'd left it unthought.

She seemed to relax. 'Very well. What would you like to see?'

He smiled. 'Well, everything, I suppose.'

'Everything? Even the root cellar?'

'Definitely the root cellar.'

She scowled and he had to fight to repress a grin. 'For goodness' sake! You can't possibly think the root cellar's important!'

He lost the battle with his grin. 'It is if you like buttered parsnips.'

Despair grew in Maddy as she showed him around, Ketch at their heels. He'd said from top to bottom, and she did just that. Everything. Kitchens, storage rooms, root cellar, the cool, tiled dairy, the old north solar that was now a library-cum-drawing room, the one-time garde tower converted to extra bedchambers; she showed him all over the house, and with every step her heart sank lower.

They went back through the hall, collected his coat and her cloak and went out through the main doors into the wind that snapped and whistled about them, down the steps to the courtyard and out to the stables. There the great shire horses that worked the fields snorted softly in greeting, and her cob, little Bunty, whiffled for the carrot she'd brought.

Ash checked on his elegant mare, who seemed comfortable enough with a pile of hay. He asked where she kept her carriage and she showed him. Not that there was a carriage, only the gig, along with the farm carts. There was, she assured him nervously, room if he wanted a proper closed carriage, and more horses. He nodded, frowning slightly.

She showed him into the walled garden with its wintry, bare vegetable beds and skeletal fruit trees, rimed with snow. He said very little, but she could tell he was taking everything in and her heart wept for this last lost chance.

Only a fool could have thought for a minute that he would be interested in Haydon at all. She had visited his home, Ravensfell Castle, with her mother once as a child. All of Haydon would fit into its outer bailey. And Ravensfell was grand, luxurious, with state apartments where Good Queen Bess had stayed on one of her progressions around the country. This—Haydon—was not what he was used to. If Good Queen Bess had even known it was here it was as much as she'd done. Perhaps he'd just come so that he could let her down gently. Or perhaps he had not really remembered Haydon at all after so many years.

The sun flickered out as she was leading him along the narrow path around the outside of the walls, high above the river. The pale light splashed briefly on the soft greyish-brown stone and was gone again. Ketch spotted a rabbit and took off after it in a silent rush. Maddy's eyes pricked and she dashed at them, shoving back a loose curl whipping her face. Beyond the wind's cry the river sang and a sheep bleated. They had stopped and were looking down over the valley, bare and bleak in its white veil. Across the valley and beyond the fells clouds loomed in heavy-laden masses. More snow. She looked at Ash. He would need to leave soon or be caught in it.

She dragged in a deep breath. Better a swift blow than a lingering agony. 'This isn't at all the sort of thing you are used to, is it?' she said, trying to keep the bitterness of despair out of her voice. She loved Haydon so much, it was hard to accept that to others, like Edward, or her brother Stephen, it was just an inconvenient, isolated pile of dressed stone.

He shook his head. 'No. Not at all.'

She nodded. 'I'm sorry. It was a stupid idea. I should have known better.'

He frowned. 'Maddy. I lived in an officer's tent on

campaign in Spain and Portugal for five years. There is nothing wrong with Haydon.'

She didn't quite believe it. 'But—Ravensfell—'

'Is Gerald's home. Not mine.' He turned and took her gloved hand. 'I don't want Ravensfell, or anything like it, even if I could afford it.'

His voice was absolute, and her heart skipped several beats as he drew her a little closer.

'Maddy, are you quite sure you don't regret that letter?'

Mute, she shook her head, staring up at him. Surely—?

'Well, in that case—' Strong hands enclosed hers, held them safe. 'It was a very nice proposal, but I find myself quite unable to accept it, so…'

She tried to pull away as pain slashed at her, but his hands tightened on hers.

'Madeleine Kirkby, will you do me the honour of accepting my hand in marriage and be my wife?'

Her heart stopped as she stared up into the sea-grey eyes. 'You'll marry me? You want Haydon?'

'I want to marry you,' he said.

They stood in a sheltered corner between two of the buttresses, out of the worst of the wind. Soon, thought Maddy, she would wake up and realise that she had been dreaming, that she was still trapped in the nightmare reality of losing Haydon and failing her people. But here and now, in this dream with its biting cold, she had—

'Maddy?'

She realised that she hadn't accepted. 'Yes. Yes, please,' she said very politely.

A sound that might have been a laugh escaped him. 'Shall we seal that in the usual way?' he suggested.

She frowned up at him. He was still holding her hands. But she supposed it was a sort of bargain between them. 'You want to shake hands on it?' She didn't imagine he'd want to spit in his palm first.

This time he definitely laughed. 'No. I've a better idea.'

Before she could even draw breath to ask what it was, he released her hands—but only to take her in his arms and bring her closer. Her breath shortened at the startling strength that surrounded her, held her. She had never been this close to a man. She had not realised that a man could be so...*hard*. Certainly she had not known it was possible to feel utterly safe and shatteringly vulnerable at the same moment.

'Maddy.' Somehow he'd shed a glove, and his bare hand was under her chin, lifting it. And not just lifting it but feathering along the line of her jaw, tracing the curve, while his thumb stroked across her lips. The shock of his touch burned through her, melting thought and scattering her wits.

Then his mouth was on hers.

She had always thought, assumed, that kissing was a

mere bumping of mouths, slightly ridiculous and possibly revolting if someone had bad teeth.

This, Ash's kiss, was not a mere anything. Nor was it ridiculous or revolting. It was a revelation. His mouth moved on hers, warm and supple, in a caress that not only stole her wits but removed all desire for their return. Feeling was enough. Tentatively, unsure of the correct thing to do, Maddy returned his kiss and gasped, fire spinning through her as his arms tightened.

Ash thought he might explode at that first shy response. Her lips were so damn soft, so sweet, as they moved hesitantly against his. Torn between the aching need for more and the restraining knowledge that she was an innocent, he touched his tongue to her lips, licked into the seam. She gasped, her lips parting, and he pressed into the honeyed sweetness, taking her mouth, tasting and teasing. Honey. Spice. Something that must be Maddy.

God help him, he'd been wanting to kiss her since seeing her in Blakiston's office the other day. He'd known he wanted to kiss her. He just hadn't known how much. He certainly hadn't had the least conception of how *her* kissing *him* would affect him. Nor had he realised just how good her slight curves would feel pressed against him. In short, he'd expected to kiss her, enjoy it and be able to let her go.

He couldn't. Not easily. With a savage effort of will he broke the kiss. His breathing harsh, he held her. Just held her. Fiercely aware of her shaken breath, the soft curves pressed against him, the burn of his blood and the ache in his groin.

Two weeks and we'll be married.

'This is going to be the longest two weeks of my life,' he said, not quite recognising the rough voice that came from him.

Maddy took a deep breath, fighting back against the wave of panic. This wasn't at all what she'd expected. Scions of ducal houses were meant to know all about marriages of convenience and what they entailed.

Marriages of convenience did not entail forbidden kisses under the walls of the castle. They did not entail finding oneself locked in Ash Ravensfell's arms and wanting to remain there for ever, pressed against his heart. They certainly should not entail this singing leap in her own blood and heart at the thought that he might want *her*, Maddy Kirkby. Not just Haydon.

He's always been kind. And...and honourable.

She let that first breath out and took another. 'You don't have to pretend pretty stories for me, Ash.' His arms hardened, but she forced herself on. 'We both know it's Haydon you want. I'm offering a marriage of convenience.'

She found herself set back from him in one swift move, his narrowed eyes boring into her as he gripped her shoulders.

'A marriage of convenience.'

She got her breath under control. Sort of. 'Yes. You don't have to pretend.'

'Pretend what? That I desire you?'

Why the devil did she have to blush? 'Yes. That. You can't—'

'Desiring the woman you plan to marry seems perfectly convenient to me.'

His voice was cool. And there was no answer to that flawless logic. Not that she could make.

He went on. 'Men do that, Maddy. Desire women. All the time. Were you envisaging a marriage in name only?'

'What?' For a moment she didn't follow his meaning. Then, 'No!' She wasn't such a ninny that she had expected that. Besides, she thought children might be rather nice one day.

'Good,' he said flatly. 'Because you wouldn't get it.' One long finger traced the line of her throat, set little flames dancing under the skin, stole her breath. 'And,' he added softly, that wicked finger finding her frantic pulse beat, stroking, 'I really can't see a problem with us desiring each other.'

Desiring each other? Was that what she felt? 'Er...'

'In fact,' he went on, as if she hadn't tried to speak, 'it makes it a great deal easier.'

She stared up at him. At the mouth, now faintly smiling, that had just kissed her senseless. All very well for him. As he'd said, men desired women all the time. And until he'd kissed her, she, too, had thought a marriage of convenience would be easy. Until she'd realised that her stupid, girlish *tendre* for him had required only one devastating kiss, one gentle caress, to flare back to inconvenient, embarrassing life.

An odd look flashed across his face. 'Ah, you *do* know what happens, don't you, Maddy?'

Her cheeks flamed. 'Of course I do! I've brought plenty of rams and bulls to tup, and...' Her breath shortened and her heart pounded as his gaze seared her. 'I...I mean, I know it's not *exactly* the same, but—' Something in his eyes silenced her.

'I think,' he said, in a tight, strained voice, 'that we've been out here as long as is safe.'

'Safe?' she asked.

'That's correct,' he said, still in that strange tone. 'You aren't safe.'

She stared. 'I'm not?'

'No. You aren't.'

Chapter Four

Ash rode back into Haydon village just as dusk was falling on the afternoon of the twenty-third. It had been snowing lightly for the past five miles, and old Runcorn, the innkeeper, welcomed him heartily, handing him a cup of hot punch.

'Come you in, my lord. All's ready. Will you be going up to the castle tonight?'

Ash gave him a narrow look as he sipped the punch gratefully. He had done his best to keep the betrothal quiet, worried that Montfort might trouble Maddy, but clearly the secret was out. 'Not tonight, Runcorn.' As it was, his sleep had been disturbed for the past two weeks with anticipatory dreams of the wedding night. Which were better than nightmares, but he'd be damned if he'd take the risk of literally anticipating his vows.

Runcorn ushered him to the stairs. 'Never you fear, m'lord. There's only a few knows what's afoot. And glad we are of it.' He shook his head. 'A bad business, thinking we'd lose the castle.'

Ash followed him up the stairs. Most of his belongings had been sent ahead to Haydon in the carriage that would carry Maddy to church on the morrow. All he had with him was a portmanteau, holding enough for the night and his wedding clothes. And the marriage settlements, which he had collected from Blakiston on his way through Newcastle.

His jaw set hard at the thought of those settlements. They would have to be signed tomorrow, before the wedding, even though they were not quite as he had instructed. In fact, not at all. And there was no time to have them changed back, even if Blakiston would have agreed. As to that, he'd had not a single logical argument to advance when the wily old solicitor had pointed out that, as Miss Maddy's trustee, he was bound both legally and morally to consider her wishes.

That might be the case, but he was going to have something to say to Maddy about this. His fingers tightened on a small object in his pocket.

The church vestry was a chilly little room, fragrant with camphor and wax. Maddy read the altered settlements through very carefully to ensure they said what she wanted them to say. Satisfied, she picked up the pen and dipped it in the ink.

Signed by me, Madeleine Henrietta Fairfax Kirkby, this twenty-fourth day of December, in the Year of our Lord eighteen hundred and sixteen.

The pen ceased its scratching and Maddy set it back in the pen-rest, careful not to drip ink on the settlement. This was much fairer than the original version. Mr Blakiston had explained the details of that document very clearly when he'd brought the settlements out to her to read through a week ago.

'You retain ownership of Haydon. Should you predecease Lord Ashton, he has only a life interest in the property, which will then pass to your eldest son, or daughter if there is no son. Should you die without heirs of your body, the trust is set up so that you may bequeath Haydon, in its entirety as you please, the bequest to be effective upon the death of Lord Ashton.'

There had been more. Every eventuality had been thought of. But the crux of the matter was that Ash had given Haydon back to her and her heirs absolutely. Under the terms of the original settlement Ash had asked Mr Blakiston to draw up, Haydon would never really be his.

She was fiercely conscious of Ash standing behind her, waiting to sign. He had barely spoken to her when she arrived, his greeting curt, his eyes as grey and cold as a winter sea. A tremor ran through her. *Heirs of your body.* She had lived in the country all her life. She knew how those heirs would be conceived. How could she not? But until Ash had kissed her she had not known that a man's touch could set her pulse awry and steal the breath from her body.

He was not angry with you then.

He was definitely angry now. With her.

He came forward, tall and straight, every movement controlled and easy. Yet his mouth was set in a hard line. Her foot caught in the hem of her gown as she rose, but before she could even stumble his hand was there, under her elbow, steadying her. Through the velvet sleeve of her gown and the leather of his glove every nerve sang at his touch and the strength in those lean fingers, even as they bit into her arm. She said nothing, but at her sharp intake of breath he released her and stepped back.

Heart pounding, she waited while Ash signed the documents, his face coldly expressionless, and his brother the duke and Mr Blakiston witnessed the signatures. There were three copies, now all formally signed and witnessed. One would be kept with Blakiston, one at Haydon and one with the Ravensfell family records to safeguard both parties to the transaction. She had to remember, no matter that Ash could set every nerve in her body alight, that it was just that: a business transaction.

It was done. She hoped.

'It…it is binding, isn't it?' she asked. 'Legally?'

Mr Blakiston nodded. 'This is your twenty-first birthday. You are of age and your marriage—' he pulled out his watch '—in half an hour will ratify the contract, bring it into force.'

The vicar, Mr Parmenter, was hovering in the background. 'Perhaps, Miss Kirkby, you might like to come back to the vicarage for a few moments. A time for solemn reflection and prayer?'

Ash spoke. 'I should like to speak to Miss Kirkby for a moment.' His voice was as hard as the gaze that held hers.

She swallowed. What had happened? They had signed the settlements. Surely he wasn't having doubts now?

She hesitated. 'Thank you, Mr Parmenter, but I should like to speak to Lord Ashton privately, please.'

The vicar frowned. Clearly leaving the bride and groom alone *before* the wedding, whatever had to happen afterwards, was not at all usual. Especially not in his vestry. Bad enough that the wedding was so hasty, and there had been this mad scramble to sign the contracts within half an hour of the wedding. He opened his mouth, probably to object.

'Of course, of course,' said the duke cheerfully. 'The duchess and I will accept your offer, Parmenter. Very kind. A cup of tea would be just the thing—wouldn't it, my lady?'

The duchess rose to the occasion. 'Indeed it would.' She shepherded the vicar out with a question about the stone carving around the font. 'Most interesting. Quite unusual. Is it Saxon?'

The door clicked shut behind the duke and they were alone.

'Why the changes to the settlements, Maddy?' His voice was clipped and hard.

Maddy frowned. Was that all that was bothering him? 'They weren't fair. Essentially they gave Haydon back to me in its entirety. Now it will belong to us jointly.'

Ash muttered something under his breath. 'Damn it, Maddy!' he went on. 'The settlements were supposed to protect you!'

'They still do,' she said. 'Now they protect you, as well. And if I die without heirs, Haydon is yours.'

Most marriage settlements ensured that any property brought by the bride ended up firmly in her husband's hands, unless her relatives or trustees insisted otherwise. Under the circumstances, having practically begged Ash to marry her, she had not made any stipulations to the contrary.

'What the devil were you thinking?' he demanded. 'Haydon should be yours, Maddy! And I don't need protecting!'

'No, but—'

'So, *why*? Why did you do it?'

'Because I wanted Haydon to be *ours*,' she said simply. 'It's more mine that way.'

His jaw dropped. 'Then perhaps my birthday gift is not as foolish as I feared,' he said, very softly. 'Here.'

He reached into his pocket and drew out something small. 'We found it together,' he said, handing it to her.

It rested in her hand. Small, solid and warm. The little bronze horse that had endured hidden for so long. Maddy's throat tightened as she saw again the bright summer's day he'd found it, the sky a wild arc of windswept blue above them, and Ash, his fingers and eyes reverent as he brushed centuries of dirt from the little figure. In a queer way it was not just a gift from Ash but from Haydon itself, to both of them.

A gift from the past to their future.

Her fingers closed over the little horse as tears pricked the backs of her eyes. 'Thank you,' she whispered, and stretched up on tiptoe to kiss him.

She was aiming for his jaw, but somehow, with a slight movement of his head, she missed. The kiss landed full on his mouth—his very willing, ready mouth—and she was in his arms. The world rocked, tilted wildly for a single mad moment, as his mouth possessed hers and his arms tightened. Every nerve, every fibre of her body sang, blazed with need. Then, with what sounded remarkably like a curse, he released her and stepped back.

'We had better,' he said carefully, 'join Gerald and Helen with the vicar.'

Ash barely noticed the church filling up behind him as he waited by the chancel steps for Maddy. She had blindsided him. And not just by the alterations to the marriage settlements. Although that was shocking enough. He'd instructed Blakiston to draw up the settlements so that Maddy was completely protected. Even from himself.

No, that wasn't what had really shocked him. What had done that was the fact that, despite all the lectures he had read himself over the past two weeks, the moment she had drawn close and he had breathed that sweet lavender and Maddy fragrance he'd been hard and aching. And when she'd touched him, reached up to kiss him, he'd been close, God help him, to making the vicar's worst fears fact.

He shoved those thoughts aside. He'd given her the little horse, a talisman he'd carried with him for years as a reminder of home. Every time he had looked at it he had been back on the fells with Maddy, the summer sun bright above them in a wide sky. He'd never thought to part with it, but this felt strangely right—she'd given him herself and a home; he'd given her the reminder.

Somehow, in giving it away, he'd kept what had always been most important about the little horse.

The stir at the back of the church, murmurs and shuffling, had him turning to look. There, bright in the dim interior of the old church, was Maddy, glowing in amber velvet, on Mr Blakiston's arm. He had not understood quite how bereft Maddy was of family until he'd realised that Blakiston would be giving her away.

Watching her now, walking towards him, her head high, he vowed to make sure she was never lonely again. That she knew she had a family. His family, and the family he hoped they would make together.

But perhaps she wasn't quite alone.... The people of Haydon filled the bride's side of the church—men, women, children and even a couple of infants in their mothers' arms. Smiles and blessings followed in her wake as she came to him at the chancel steps.

'Dearly beloved—'

The vicar began the marriage service, and the familiar words washed over Maddy. So many times she had stood in this church for the wedding of one of her people. Now it was her turn. Soon she would be married. Haydon would be safe.

She glanced sideways at Ash and felt the shattering leap of her heart at the sight of him, tall and strong beside her.

'...is not by any to be enterprised, nor taken in hand, unadvisedly, lightly or wantonly, to satisfy men's carnal lusts and appetites, like brute beasts that have no understanding, but reverently, discreetly, advisedly, soberly...'

Heat stole across her cheeks. *Reverent* and *sober* were about the last words applicable to the way Ash had kissed her. Hopefully the warning meant that marriage was not to be entered into *only* to satisfy carnal lusts....

'Therefore if any man can show any just cause, why they may not lawfully be joined together, let him now speak, or else hereafter for ever hold his peace.'

The vicar paused and glanced around the church. He drew breath and continued, 'I require and charge you both, as ye will answer at the dreadful day of judgement when the secrets of all hearts shall be disclosed, that if either of you know any impediment—'

The west door crashed open.

'Stop!'

Shock slammed into her, along with the blast of cold air. Stunned, she turned. Edward was striding down the nave, flanked by two of his men.

The vicar drew himself up. 'Lord Montfort—'

'The marriage cannot go ahead,' announced Edward. 'I forbid it.'

Maddy's temper flashed. 'You cannot forbid it. I am of age, and—'

She found herself set gently aside. Ash had stepped forward, placing himself between her and Edward.

'This is for me to deal with, Maddy,' he said quietly. Facing Edward, he said, 'You've no power to forbid it, Montfort. Madeleine is of full age to consent to marriage.'

'She is promised to *me*,' declared Edward.

Furious, Maddy stepped forward, avoiding Ash's arm when he would have held her back. 'No, I am *not*!'

Edward ignored her. 'She was promised to me and got in a huff when I glanced sideways at some worthless dairymaid. It was nothing, but she became upset, and—'

'Unfaithful *before* the wedding, Montfort?' put in the duke from the front pew. 'A little unwise, wouldn't you say?'

The duchess looked disapproving.

Edward gritted his teeth. 'An indiscretion. One that won't happen again. The fact remains that Madeleine is promised to me.'

'Witnesses?' snapped Ash.

Maddy went cold. Why was he asking for witnesses? Surely—*surely*—he didn't *believe* this nonsense?

Edward smiled as if he scented victory, and gestured to the men with him. 'These fellows heard my proposal and Madeleine's acceptance. They'll swear to it.'

Under Maddy's hand Ash tensed, the muscles in his arm rigid. 'Really? You offered marriage in front of two of your...henchmen.' His lip curled. 'That must have been a romantic moment. I, on the other hand, have a letter in Miss Kirkby's hand agreeing to marriage.'

His eyes narrowed, Edward said, 'My proposal predates your letter!'

Ash snorted. 'Of course it does. Probably so does Miss Kirkby's refusal!'

'She's promised to *me*!' Edward's roar rang in the vaulted space of the church.

'The hell she is!' snarled Ash. His hand covered Maddy's, clamping over it.

Maddy found her voice. 'Edward, I never agreed to marry you or gave you any hope that I would marry you.' Fury spat from her. 'In fact, I wouldn't marry you if my life depended on it!'

His eyes hardened. 'Think carefully, Madeleine, before you defy me.'

Fury ripped through her. 'I don't have to think, Edward. I know what you are, and I refused your offer!'

He lowered his voice. 'You could be carrying my child.'

He hadn't lowered his voice enough. A shocked silence gripped the church, followed by a surge of gasps and chatter.

Maddy's stomach roiled. 'Your—?'

Ash's fist crashed into Edward's jaw.

Montfort staggered back, wheezing as Ash followed his right to the jaw with a left straight to the solar plexus.

The vicar's wail of 'Gentlemen!' barely penetrated the red-hazed battle fury hammering in every vein as he blocked a punch from Montfort and ploughed his own fist back into the bastard's face.

Montfort went down in a crashing tangle with the lectern and stayed down, blood dripping from his nose.

Ash strode forward, fully intending to haul Montfort up just for the pleasure of knocking him down again. Several times. Somehow Gerald was in the way.

His brother's calm voice steadied him. 'I'd say he's had enough, wouldn't you?' And Gerald poked the earl with his shoe. Poked hard enough for the gesture to qualify as a kick. 'Why don't we remove him so we can get on with the wedding?' His hand gripped Ash's arm and he spoke softly. 'The wedding, Ash. That's the important thing now. *Think*, lad.'

'Ash?'

Maddy's voice sliced through him. He turned, and on her face he saw fear.

'Ash—please…'

He strode to her, caught her hands. 'Not here, Maddy. Later.'

She stared up at him, her hands trembling in his. Doubts whispered. Could it be true? Oh, not that she had gone to Montfort willingly, but that he had thought to force her hand, disgrace her so that she could not wed?

And she didn't tell you?

He fought for control. How the hell could a woman tell a man *that*? Especially a man she didn't know very well. When it might mean losing her home and failing people dependent on her. And there were things he had not told *her*—his nightmares.

So what now? His hands tightened on hers. Leaving her at the altar was unthinkable. Nor could he demand an explanation. Not here. Not now. If he showed the least hesitation in marrying Maddy, the story would spread, grow in the telling. She'd be ruined, a social pariah. He couldn't do that to her. Any explanations would have to come later. Right now, at least until they were utterly alone, he would behave as though there could not be the least doubt that Montfort was a lying bastard.

And if she is carrying his child?

He shoved the thought away. Protecting Maddy trumped any other consideration. He'd worry about that later.

A throat being cleared got his attention. Several of Maddy's men had come forward, Brady at their head.

'We'll handle this lying scum, my lord.' Brady's face was grim as he and two others bent down and dragged Montfort to his feet.

Ash's hands tightened on Maddy's as he reined in the urge to smash a fist or two into Montfort's jaw again. 'Thank you.' It came out between gritted teeth.

'Be a right pleasure,' said Brady. With a total lack of

ceremony, Montfort and his companions were bundled from the church.

His decision made, Ash faced the vicar, still with Maddy's hands clasped in his. 'Continue, sir.'

Parmenter spluttered. 'Well, as to that, my lord…er… it might be better to…ah, wait on events…as it were. I really couldn't in all conscience—'

'Parmenter.' Ash spoke with a lethal softness. 'If you will not continue the service, I will have no choice but to convey Miss Kirkby to Ravensfell and marry her there. I will not allow Montfort's lies—' *please, God, they were lies* '—to ruin this day.'

Blakiston spoke up. 'Mr Parmenter, if Lord Montfort had truly gained Miss Kirkby's consent to marriage, then I would have been asked to draw up marriage settlements for them. I assure you he lied.'

The vicar let out a breath. 'That may be, but the other accusation—' His face reddened. 'The suggestion of unchastity—'

'Is a matter between myself and Miss Kirkby,' said Ash. 'It is not for any other to judge.' He flung all decorum to the winds. 'Even if I did entertain the least doubt of Miss Kirkby's virtue, do you imagine that *I* am a virgin?'

There were quite a few muffled laughs in the church, quickly stifled as Parmenter whipped around to glare at the impious.

'Well…' The vicar settled his preaching bands. 'If your lordship's mind is made up—'

'It is.'

Parmenter cleared his throat, took up his position and began to read again. 'I require and charge you both—'

Chapter Five

Maddy got through the rest of the service in a daze. From a distance she heard Ash promise to love and cherish her. His voice was very clear, his hand clasping hers firmly. And then she was repeating her own vows, her voice shaking on the word *love*. *Love*. So easily promised. How many couples meant it? Really meant it and kept to it?

He had married her in the teeth of Edward's accusations. Dismissed them publicly as lies.

He vowed to honour you. He has already done it.

Her heart, already besieged, shook a little at the knowledge that he had trusted her without question.

Then Ash was slipping the ring onto her finger, holding it there. 'With this ring I thee wed, with my body I thee worship…'

His gaze held hers and she felt the heat swirling through her.... *With my body...* Another vow. Spoken in a way that left no doubt he fully intended to keep it.

At last it was over, and they left the church to wildly pealing bells and heavy pewter skies.

The duke and duchess took their leave swiftly after a glass of wine in the vicarage. 'We simply can't stay any longer if we are to reach home and our guests tonight,' said the duchess, pressing Maddy's hand in farewell. 'Do say you forgive us, and will come after Twelfth Night.' She smiled. 'Ash is very wise to keep you all to himself for now. Ravensfell will be quieter then, with most of our guests gone and just our sons and Gerald and Ash's sisters for another week. They are all looking forward to seeing you.'

Maddy stammered a thank-you and the duchess leaned forward to kiss her on the cheek. 'And don't worry about Montfort's idiocy. He's done himself a very great deal of harm, if he only knew it.'

Her cheeks burned. 'Madam, it was all—'

'Helen,' the duchess corrected her. 'And you don't need to tell me it was all lies. His mother always did spoil him dreadfully, and just see what has come of it!' She patted Maddy's hand. 'Oh, dear. Poor Gerald is positively glaring at me from the door! I must go. Merry Christmas, my dear!' She turned to Ash, fixing him with what she possibly imagined was a severe look. 'Behave yourself.'

The duke strolled up and caught his duchess's hand, sliding it onto his arm. 'Not precisely the advice to give a man on his wedding day, m'dear.' He smiled at Maddy, who was wondering if she'd heard right. 'I'll just wish you very happy again.' He cast a sideways look at his own wife. 'And assure you that he's highly unlikely to take Helen's bit of advice to heart, luckily for you.'

Apparently she had heard correctly. The Duke of Thirlmere had a very wicked twinkle in his eye, even as the duchess thumped his shoulder.

'Thank you, brother,' said Ash in carefully restrained tones. 'Just what advice would you give me on my wedding night?'

The duke raised his brows. 'I'd be surprised to learn you needed any.' He frowned. 'Actually, there is something—leave Montfort to me.'

And he was gone before Ash could do more than open his mouth.

The vicar gulped. 'Ah, more claret, Lord Ashton? Ratafia, Lady Ashton?'

Ash handed his bride into the carriage Gerald had lent him—*'Just until you can arrange your own'*—to the accompaniment of enthusiastic cheers and with a restraint that had his jaw aching. At some point he was going to have to know the truth—if Montfort had forced Maddy, or even attempted to. The thought that Maddy, *his* Maddy, might have suffered that sickened him. As for Gerald's advice to leave Montfort to him—his brother had rocks in his head.

He stepped into the carriage, fishing in his coat pocket for the coins he'd put there. Leaning out, he flung the coins into the crowd of villagers, who scooped them up, still cheering.

As the carriage lurched off he settled himself on the seat opposite Maddy and saw that she had the carriage rug tucked around her as well as her cloak. 'Are you warm enough?'

She nodded. 'Yes. There are hot bricks under my feet, too.' Her eyes met his shyly. 'I think they are intended for both of us, and the rug is quite large enough to share.'

Ash's body had an instant and predictable reaction to the suggestion that he share the rug with Maddy. 'I'm warm enough,' he said. *Too damned warm.* And he hadn't meant to sound like a bear with a spike in its paw.

'Oh.' She went a little pink. 'Er…that was very generous of you,' she said. 'The coins. But most of the people from the castle had gone. I mean, they weren't there to—'

He managed a smile despite the nagging ache in his groin. Typical of Maddy to think of her people. 'I have more for them. And I thought we would add something to everyone's wages to celebrate our marriage.'

Her face changed. 'It nearly wasn't,' she said softly, leaning forward.

He tried not to breathe, but the soft scent of lavender and Maddy wound about and through him and he reached for her hand, enveloped it in his. 'Nearly wasn't what?'

'A celebration.' A trembling smile ripped at his heart. 'You married me despite what Edward did.' Her fingers tightened on his.

What Edward did?

He floundered for words to explain that he knew, whatever had happened, it hadn't been her fault. That he'd never blame—

Her mouth brushed against his—the merest promise of a kiss, a feather of a kiss.

'Thank you.'

The soft words breathed against his lips and he was lost. When she pulled back his arms closed about her gently and he was on the wrong side of the carriage, on the seat beside her, sanity incinerated as desire ignited. There were reasons he shouldn't be doing this. In some distant corner of his brain he knew that. He was supposed to be talking to her. Reassuring her. But he no longer cared. With a groan Ash released the death grip he'd imposed on his self-control and kissed her instead.

Her mouth was a miracle of sweetness, soft and yielding under the demands of his, kissing him back. He wanted that. He wanted everything. Everything and more. Wanted the shy touch of her tongue, stroking against his, the spicy Maddy taste of her, the silk of her hair as he disposed of her bonnet and slid his fingers into the fragrant curls. Hairpins pattered on the leather squabs and to the floor as her hair tumbled free around her shoulders, coiling, twining around his fingers like living silk.

Nothing else mattered. Just Maddy. In his arms, giving herself freely until he could scarcely breathe for wanting her. Under the heavy pelisse he found the slender, supple curve of her waist encased in velvet, the gentle swell of her breast above. She stilled and he deepened the kiss, cupping her breast through velvet and her stays. Heat hammered in his veins as he traced the tender curve of her breast beneath the confining material.

His mouth consumed a soft gasp and he was lost in the kiss, in her. Swiftly he unbuttoned the pelisse, slipped it from her shoulders and sank back into the enchantment.

Too many clothes and he needed to touch *her*, touch Maddy. His body on fire, he stroked down one leg, over the richness of velvet—and slid beneath, her skirts rucked over his arm. She gasped as he caressed her knee, as his fingers slid higher and found warm, bare skin that shamed silk and velvet....

* * *

Struggling for breath, Maddy pulled back from the kiss.

'Ash!'

Somehow she found the breath for his name, stunned at the intimacy of his touch there on her thigh. Stroking, maddening, on her inner thigh. Higher he slid, and higher, until she wanted to scream with need.

There! Higher... Please!

Somewhere, someone made a frantic little noise and his hand withdrew. She realised that she had cried out and nearly wept in frustration.

'Do you want me to stop?' His voice, tight and strained, sounded exactly as she felt.

'No. Please. No.'

The words were barely out before his mouth took hers again, complete and deep.

Madness took Ash. Never breaking the kiss, he lifted her over him so that she straddled his thighs, petticoats and skirts spilling over him in a froth of velvet and muslin.

Slipping his hand back under her skirts, he found her, hot and damp, and consumed the frantic little cry of shock as he explored the melting folds. For an instant she was utterly still in his arms, and then on a moan she pushed against him, her body pleading, begging for more, her mouth frantic on his as he stroked.

Her body was no longer hers, but his to command. Thought was long gone. There was only the ache in her breasts and the deepening ache in her belly and lower, where he touched her with such shattering intimacy, there where she was open to him. And his kiss—all dark heat—the surge of his tongue, taking her mouth in the same possessive rhythm as his wicked fingers between her thighs.

He should stop. He knew that. But instead he was unbuttoning the fall of his pantaloons, freeing himself. His mouth devouring hers, he guided himself to her entrance, gripping her hip with his free hand as he eased her down to meet the savage ache of his erection. Liquid silk spilled over him, over his fingers, and he fought not to just take her. He eased in a little farther, shaking, burning… So tight, so hot and wet… And then he felt it. Not just tightness. A resistance that could mean only one thing.…

His mind fought free for an instant of the heat engulfing him.

Not like this. It shouldn't be like this!

'Maddy, no. Wait, sweetheart!' His voice was harsh, scarcely recognisable to himself.

But she squirmed against him, pressing down, sobbing in a wordless plea. And his body responded, thrusting upwards into the welcoming warmth, his mouth taking her shocked cry as he breached her maidenhead and slid deep into paradise.

Pain cut, sharp and swift, and Maddy fought for breath, slowly realising that although he was buried inside her, Ash wasn't moving at all. That his fingers were clamped like a vice on her hips, holding her still. She couldn't believe how *stretched* she felt. How deep he was inside her. She took a careful breath, not entirely sure there was room inside her for anything other than him.

'*Don't move.*'

She froze. The words sounded as though they'd been chipped out of solid granite. His breath was harsh in her ear.

'Are you all right?'

She wondered if he was in pain, his voice was so rough. 'No. Yes. I...' She tried another breath. 'I don't know.'

But even as she spoke she realised that the pain had faded, was only memory, leaving behind a restless need to *move*, to ease the ache.

He spoke again. 'I'm sorry. I shouldn't have—'

His voice broke off as she moved, and his fingers gripped savagely. She tightened around him on a gasp.

'Damn.'

He groaned and began to move beneath her, hard and fast. There was no pain now; her body was flaming to life as he thrust again and again. Need, pressure coiled and built. Dimly she heard a frantic voice, sobbing, pleading, and realised *she* was sobbing, *she* was pleading.... And then his body hardened as he groaned, thrust up into her and held still and deep, shuddering as warmth flooded her. She took a shaky breath, aching with need as she understood—it was finished...he was spent.

Very slowly, Ash returned to his wits. *Maddy.* He'd taken Maddy's virginity in a damned carriage. Gently, he lifted her from him. Hell's teeth! She had deserved better than that for her first time. Deserved better than to be deflowered in a carriage by a bridegroom who, for whatever reason, had doubted her innocence. She had deserved a bed and a man who had at least taken care to satisfy her before taking his own selfish pleasure. And if he had been right about Montfort then she had deserved those things all the more!

'Here.' He handed her his handkerchief. She stared at it and he said carefully, 'You might like it to...cleanse yourself.'

'Oh.' Crimson flooded her cheeks.

Tactfully, he looked away while she dealt with matters and he put himself back together.

'Thank you for the handkerchief,' she said at last.

He turned to look at her. She was still pink, her hair tumbling wildly about her shoulders, her eyes uncertain.

'Are you all right?' He'd hurt her, and the knowledge ate at him.

'I— Yes.'

He swallowed. 'Sweetheart, it will get better. It was only because it was your first time. I should have waited—if I'd known—' He broke off, realising what he'd implied.

'But...you *did* know.' Then, with dawning horror, 'Didn't you?'

He shut his eyes. He could only hope that when his wits returned from wherever they'd gone begging he would know what to do with them.

The truth crashed over Maddy. He had thought she wasn't a virgin.

'You believed Edward,' she whispered. It felt like breathing broken glass. 'How could you think that I would have let him—?'

'I thought he probably hadn't given you much choice,' said Ash, his voice very quiet. 'Maddy, it wouldn't have been your fault.'

'But you thought I'd deceived you.' She dragged in a breath. 'That I hadn't told you.'

'Damn it, Maddy!' His voice was tight. 'I didn't think you'd *deceived* me, just that—'

He reached for her, but she jerked back. 'No. Don't touch me. Why did you marry me if you thought—?'

'That he'd forced you?' The ugly word was matched by his harsh voice. 'To protect you, of course!'

'Even though you thought I was deliberately deceiving you?' Bitterness welled up. 'You must really have wanted Haydon.'

Grey eyes narrowed to blazing slits. His hands shot out, gripped her shoulders, forcing a gasp from her.

'You were the one who changed the settlements, Maddy,' he ground out. 'My version left Haydon entirely in your hands. Is that the action of a man who wanted your property? And I didn't see it as deception! You were trying to protect your home, your people.' He let out a breath, releasing her, and said quietly, 'I didn't like it, but I understood.'

She couldn't think. Logic was beyond her, so she didn't answer at all. Instead, fingers trembling with hurt, fury, a nameless ferment of emotion, Maddy fumbled with the hairpins remaining to her and forced some order into her unruly locks. She snatched her bonnet up and jammed it back on, but the bonnet ribbons defeated her.

'Here.'

Ash reached over and she pulled back as his fingers grazed her throat, flinching at the leap of her pulse.

'Sit still and I'll tie them for you.'

His voice was harsh. Wonderful. Not only did he think her capable of deceiving him, he thought her incapable of putting on a simple bonnet. She sat still, shutting her eyes to block out the sight of him so close to her.

Snow swirled down in great soft flakes as the carriage rumbled through the main gate into the outer bailey. A shout went up and a lad dashed out to help as the horses drew to a halt.

The door opened and Brady looked in. 'Here y'are. I'll get that.' He bent and set the steps down, and stood back, holding the door. 'Welcome, m'lord.' He cast a glance at the flakes drifting down from the leaden sky. 'I'd say yeh made it just in time.'

Maddy bit her lip. It probably wasn't quite the decorous formality Ash was used to in a ducal household, but he just smiled, as if they hadn't travelled the last mile in a frozen silence, and stepped down.

'Thank you, Brady.'

'Yeh're welcome, m'lord.'

Ash held out his hands for Maddy. She made to put her hands in his to step down, but he set his hands to her waist.

'Ash! No, I'm too—'

She was lifted with an effortless strength that bobbled the breath from her lungs, and found herself cradled in his arms. Heat curled and tightened in her belly, tingled beneath her skin as his knowing gaze caressed her.

'Too what, my lady?' he challenged her, and strode towards the inner bailey. He crossed it without hesitation and made straight for the stairs.

At the foot of the stairs lay an enormous log, and Maddy's heart leaped. She looked over her shoulder at Brady bringing up the rear. 'Is that—?'

'The Yule log, m'lady.' His grin lit his face. 'Didn't think we'd miss that, did yeh?'

She swallowed. 'We weren't going to bother.' There had seemed no point, with Edward taking possession the day after Twelfth Night.

If Ash hadn't married me, we'd all be packing.

'But things is different now,' said Brady. 'Go on up, m'lord and lady. They're waitin' for yeh.'

Maddy gulped. 'Ash, hadn't I better walk—?'

'Save your breath and don't wriggle,' he advised. His arms tightened and he started up.

Ash trod carefully up the stairs, Maddy's slight weight in his arms a blessed distraction from the guilt. Greet her people, thank them, and then they could be private over dinner while he sorted out the mess he'd made of everything.

Cheers erupted around them as he stepped across the threshold, Maddy still in his arms, and he stood stock-still, blinking. The great hall, which had been dim and peaceful that last time he was here, was full of people. A fire blazed in the hearth, all the wall sconces were lit and several branches of candles shimmered on the refectory table.

The hall breathed, simply shouted, *Christmas is come!* Ivy hung everywhere in great swathes and festoons, twisted among the roof beams. Holly, its berries gleaming scarlet, surrounded the windows, was even draped artistically around the old swords by the fireplace. Pots of rosemary stood here and there, and the vanilla fragrance of bays drifted on the air.

From the stairs leading down to the kitchen, other fragrances wafted up. Fragrances that made him realise breakfast had been a very long time ago. And the candles—candles everywhere. In the window embrasures, glimmering on an old oak coffer. Light and joy everywhere, dancing and glowing in the eyes of Haydon's people.

One look at Maddy's dazed eyes, suddenly bright with tears, told him she was just as surprised as he was.

He looked around.

'Go on, m'lord,' urged Brady.

Ash obliged, walking farther in the hall.

'That'll do nicely, lad!' yelled someone. 'Now look up!'

He did. Straight at a kissing bough that looked as though several forests' worth of oak trees must have been stripped to furnish it with mistletoe.

His breath caught.

Slowly, deliberately, he set Maddy on her feet, keeping one arm around her. His blood hammered in his veins as he reached up with his free hand and plucked a berry. He hoped to God that this time he could make sure a simple kiss remained just that—a kiss.

'I think, madam wife,' he said in a voice that reached only her, 'that you are under a misconception about my reasons for marriage.'

'Am I?' she whispered.

'Yes. Perhaps this will help you understand.'

He drew her closer and time slowed as her slender curves fitted to his as if she were made for him. Gently, he traced the delicate line of her throat, felt a tremor rack her as with a soft sigh she slipped her arms about him and yielded her mouth to his.

Ash's head spun at the sweetness of the kiss. Caring nothing for their audience, he kissed her deeply, possessively, moulding her body to his, one hand buried in the coiling silk of her hair. Time slowed, stretched into a glowing infinity of promise and delight.

'D'ye reckon it's the mistletoe?' whispered an awed voice.

Maddy's mind spun as Ash eased back from the kiss

and smiled down at her. Her breath hitched at the tenderness in those grey eyes.

'There was something I wanted more than Haydon,' he murmured.

He had wanted her? Desire, yes. But had he actually wanted *her*? Maddy? Enough to marry her despite Edward's lies?

'Wassail!' roared someone from the back of the hall, and the crowd took up the chant.

From somewhere an indecently large cup was produced, filled with hot spiced ale and passed to Maddy. She took the first sip and spluttered. Ash took it from her and deliberately set his lips where hers had rested. Their eyes met. Burned. He drank. His fingers tightened on the cup and, his eyes never leaving hers, he passed it on.

The cup was passed around until everyone had tasted it.

Ash's plans had included meeting Maddy's household as her husband and then dinner. Not an extended dinner.

He had reckoned without her household. He'd never realised that here in this isolated spot they adhered to the old tradition of the entire household eating in the hall. And, since it was Christmas Eve, after they'd hauled in the Yule log there was dancing to the lilt of Brady's old fiddle and his daughter's flute.

It was nearly ten o'clock before the hall was clear of

revellers and Maddy's housekeeper bustled her off to the bedchamber.

Ash reined in his impatience as he sat down at the table. He'd blundered in every way possible in the carriage. He was damned if he'd repeat the mistake.

Chapter Six

~~~~~~~~~~~~~~~~

Maddy had never realised that Bets had a romantic streak at all, let alone one a mile wide. She was tenderly arraying Maddy in her very prettiest lace-edged nightgown, despite her protests that it was nowhere near warm enough for a winter's night.

Bets smirked as she twitched the linen sleeve of the nightgown just so. 'Never you mind that, Miss Maddy—m'lady, I *should* say, I reckon his lordship'll keep you warm enough and to spare.'

She twisted her hands together in her lap while Bets brushed out her hair, long sweeps of the brush. It wasn't like that at all. Was it?

He had believed Edward!

As if Bets had read her mind, she said, 'Not many

men who'd have married you after what Lord Montfort said. Not without they waited to see if you was breeding.'

Maddy's hands stilled. If he'd thought Edward had… Her stomach churned. If Ash had thought that, then he must have considered the possibility that she *was* carrying a child. Edward's child. She'd been too hurt by his apparent mistrust to think that through clearly.

And he still married you…why?

Shame flooded her. He'd answered that in the carriage—*to protect you, of course!*

Straight after she'd accused him of marrying her because he'd wanted Haydon.

He did trust you, you ninnyhammer! Trusted you enough to know that you wouldn't have gone to Edward willingly. And he cared enough to marry you despite the possibility you might be pregnant. To protect you.

The little bronze horse caught her gaze in the mirror. She'd set it on the shelf over the fireplace. *He cared enough to give you that.*

Bets was still speaking. 'Someone ought to warn you.'

Warn her?

She looked at Bets in the mirror. The old woman had her mouth primmed. 'Been a long time, it has. I've been a widow longer than I was married. But you don't forget, and seeing as how your own mam, God bless her, ain't here to tell you what's what—'

Maddy's cheeks scorched. 'Um, I do know what happens, Bets,' she got out. Far better than she was going to confess.

Bets snorted. 'That's as may be, Miss Maddy. I know you'd know what goes where. Thing is, it might hurt a bit at first.'

'Oh.' Her cheeks were probably going to ignite. 'I see.'

Bets brushed harder. 'Yes. But only the first time, usually.' A very womanly smile softened the old lips. 'And 'specially with a man like his lordship. You can see he's the gentle sort, for all his strength.'

'Only the first time?' asked Maddy, trying to ignore the ache in her breasts at the thought of just how gentle Ash could be.

'Aye. After that—' Bets laid down the brush and cleared her throat. 'Well, you'll see soon enough, judging by the way his lordship can't take his eyes off you.'

Maddy realised in disbelief that Bets was blushing. Their eyes met in the mirror.

'It ain't every man who can set a girl's knees wobbling and toss her wits out the window with one kiss under the mistletoe!' Bets set her hands on Maddy's shoulders. Gave them a squeeze. 'Well. That's that. I'll be off to me bed.'

Maddy blinked and flapped a hand at her hair. 'You aren't going to braid it?'

Bets shook her head. 'Waste of time.' She twitched the neckline of the nightgown just so. 'Mind you, so's this.' Her eyes twinkled. 'But at least he'll have the fun of taking it off.'

Maddy's jaw dropped. Naked? They were going to do what they'd done in the carriage *naked*?

When she heard his knock on the door, Maddy was behind the screen, washing her face and hands. 'Come in!' She set the ewer down with trembling hands.

The door opened. Closed.

'Maddy?'

She hauled in a breath. 'Here. Behind the screen.'

'Ah.'

She leaned against the washstand, breathing carefully, shocked to realise that she was trembling. Nerves, she told herself. Perhaps he wouldn't want to do it again? A very faint hope. Most bulls and rams after a suitable rest, say half an hour or so, were more than happy to perform their duty again.

She stiffened her spine. She couldn't hide here all night, even if she *had* made a fool of herself. With a deep breath, she walked out from behind the screen to face her husband.

Her mouth dried at the sight. *Oh, Lord!* He had already dispensed with coat and waistcoat, and the lacings of his shirt hung loose, revealing the merest glimpse of a powerfully muscled chest. She swallowed, watching helplessly as he prepared to pull it off over his head, feeling again that dizziness, the aching emptiness that he had caused—and filled—in the carriage.

His gaze caught hers and he stopped.

'Would you rather I undressed somewhere else, sweetheart?' he asked. 'Behind that screen?'

The idiotish, cowardly part of her shrieked, *Yes!* Then she could dive into the bed and shut her eyes. 'No. Unless…unless you would rather?' Perhaps he thought it was immodest for her to be here? To watch.

He shook his head, a very wicked smile curving his lips. 'Not at all. I'm more than happy to strip for your pleasure.' The smile became even more wicked. 'Perhaps tomorrow night you'll return the favour.'

She was conscious of the heat, the wetness between her legs. Knew what it meant. Did he mean that *he* would find it arousing, watching her undress? Her knees shook at the thought, and prudently she backed up to lean against the high, old-fashioned bed.

'I…um…' He was unlacing his shirt fully, one hole at a time. 'I have to apologise.'

He looked at her. 'For what?'

'For…for the things I said. In the carriage.' She swallowed. 'I know that you trusted me. There's no excuse for what I said about you marrying me for Haydon because that was exactly what I offered you. I'm sorry.'

'And will you accept *my* apology?' he asked quietly. 'Not just for thinking you might not have told me everything, but for rushing you in the carriage? My excuse is pathetic—I wanted you too much.'

'You *wanted* me?'

'Oh, yes.' His gaze caressed her as he finished unlacing his shirt. Stole her breath. 'And I want you now.'

'Oh.' Her voice failed her. So they were going to...

Thought failed as well, but his smile told her he knew exactly what she would have thought if her mind hadn't melted. Still wearing the smile, he hauled his shirt off over his head and dropped it.

She had seen statues of the nude male body. Of course she had. Secretly she had doubted that the real thing could be quite as godlike as the sculptors seemed to suggest.... The sculptors, she realised, had indeed not got it quite right. For one thing they had not the advantage of working with living flesh and gleaming supple skin. With swells of muscle that bunched as a man bent to remove stockings and shoes. With firelight that shadowed every angle and danced lovingly on every hard plane. And nor could blind marble eyes possibly blaze with heat as his did as she gazed, riveted, while he unbuttoned the fall of his breeches....

Her eyes widened as he slid off the breeches and his drawers. Apparently the sculptors had got something else wrong, too. No statue she had ever seen had looked remotely like *that*. There wasn't a fig leaf in the world big enough.

He had gone very still. 'It won't hurt again, Maddy,' he said quietly. 'My word on it.'

Was the man a mind reader? 'It wasn't that,' she lied. Or not entirely that.

'No? What, then?'

Oh, Lord! 'Well, I haven't seen a real one before,' she said, desperately. 'Only statues.' She thought about it. Not quite true. 'At least, not a *man's* pizzle,' she said, feeling her cheeks heat.

They heated even more as his eyes widened and an unholy amusement curved his mouth.

'Pizzle?' he repeated in a very neutral voice, and she knew, just *knew*, she'd said the wrong thing.

Gritting her teeth, she said, 'I take it you don't call it that?'

He shook his head. 'No,' he said, in the sort of voice that suggested he was trying very hard not to laugh. 'That's a little…agricultural.'

'Well, what *is* it called, then?' she demanded.

He grinned outright. 'We'll get to that. Right now—' his gaze heated '—I'm much more interested in making love again. And this time we're going to do it properly.'

Properly? 'Didn't we do it properly before?' she asked. 'I mean, I didn't know what—'

'You did it properly,' he assured her. 'I didn't.'

She blinked. She'd brought enough bulls, rams and the occasional horse to tup to know that it was perfectly possible she was already carrying his child. Surely that constituted doing it properly?

'But—'

'Properly, Maddy.'

His voice was a promise. Or a threat, depending on how you viewed the blaze in his eyes.

'Or perhaps,' he murmured, coming towards her, 'I should say we're going to do it *improperly. Extremely* improperly.'

Definitely a threat. Her breath lodged in her throat as he set his fingers to the buttons of her nightgown and began to undo them. Button by button, he undid the nightgown, undid *her*, until the gown hung open and her heart beat a frantic tattoo against her ribs.

Ash's mouth dried at the sight as he reached for control. For the strength not to simply rip the gown from her, throw her on the bed and ravish her. That prim, demure, lace-edged linen gown was possibly the most erotic thing he'd ever seen. He steadied his breathing. Light and shadow played over her, over the half-revealed sweetness of delicately curved breasts, the slender sweep of her waist and the swell of her hips. Hands shaking, he pushed the gown from her shoulders.

She gave a startled gasp as it pooled on the bed, leaving her naked to the waist. In a defensive gesture, her arms came up to shield her breasts.

He smiled and encircled her wrists gently. 'Are you going to be shy with me?'

She flushed and bit her lip so that he immediately wanted to nip at it just there himself. Nip it and soothe it with his tongue. He leaned forward and kissed her.

He was lost in wonder as he kissed his way down her throat, heard the gasps and moans she tried to hold back. She lost the battle as his mouth closed gently over her breast and he sucked. She arched on a moan and he bit with exquisite care.

His control nearly broke at the soft scream, but he hung on. This time she was going to have everything he could give her before he took her. Every pleasure, every delight. Slowly, he released her breast, eased back, straightened.

Her eyes opened, and she looked down at his hand, tanned against the cream silk of her breast, his fingers gentle on the damp pink nipple.

'May I touch you?' she asked softly.

His lungs locked at the husky tone in her voice. 'Please.'

One small hand reached out, and she traced the curve of his shoulder, trailed her fingertips along his biceps, igniting fires in their wake. He gritted his teeth and hung on to his sanity while she discovered his chest. One finger circled a nipple, and he groaned as it tightened.

'Ash?' Uncertainty quivered in her voice and the fingertip slowed.

'Don't stop,' he told her. He didn't care if it killed him.

'Oh.' The fingertip took up its travels again. 'You kissed me. There.'

His mind blanked. That probably *would* kill him. 'I'd like that, too.' And he took a death grip on his control as her wet, warm mouth closed over his nipple. She bit very gently and he groaned at the fierce pleasure.

'Is there anything else you'd like?' she whispered against his hungry flesh.

Aching, he grasped her hand, led it lower.

'There?' she whispered.

'Oh, yes,' he breathed. And then stopped breathing as she stroked his straining length, explored him with a shy curiosity that nearly unmanned him.

Shaking, he closed her fingers around him, showed her how to reduce him to burning, savage need.

'Enough,' he said at last, and eased her hand away, clamping down on the urge to tumble her back and simply take her.

Instead, he slid to his knees before her and tugged gently at the nightgown still caught under her bottom, his eyes never leaving hers. 'Lift up for me, Maddy.'

She obeyed, and he slipped the nightgown from beneath her. It fell to the floor, God knew where. He had eyes and thought only for the delight before him.

He set his hands to her knees and, ignoring her gasp, pressed them gently apart, exposing her fully to his gaze.

'You're *looking* at me,' she said in a high, shocked voice.

'Yes.' His whole body was an aching mass of need, but he reined it back. 'And I'm going to do a great deal more than look.'

Not giving her time to think, let alone ask questions, he leaned forward and kissed her belly. The soft skin flickered and bunched under his caress, and he slid a finger into the dimple of her navel, probing gently.

Maddy couldn't think, only feel, as that finger played in her navel, the movement matching the pulsing ache between her legs so that her body shifted in restless need. His hand shifted away, lower, and was replaced by his mouth, his tongue, swirling wet, hot circles on her quivering flesh. Fire danced and burned along each nerve at the wet probe of his tongue as his fingers slid over her inner thighs, teasing, seeking. All strength fell from her and she collapsed back onto the bed as his tongue left her navel, as he bit gently at her shivering belly and his coaxing fingers found the damp secrets between her thighs. His fingers stroked, teased and seduced.

Shock seared every nerve, every fibre, as his warm breath drifted along her thigh. His breath, the nip of his teeth and the sweep of his tongue, traced the path his teasing fingers had blazed, and where they stroked now...

He wasn't... He couldn't... He did, and her mind fractured as his mouth closed over her in the most shockingly intimate kiss. Heat speared her—dark, demanding heat—as his mouth and tongue ripped the world away. One arm lay in heavy possession across her waist, holding her there helpless while he pleasured her.

Slowly, carefully, he penetrated her with one finger, and she tightened around him, frantic, urgent. Another finger and her body bucked against the searing delight. He pressed up and found something inside her, something that exploded fireworks behind her eyelids, drove pleasure through her body, forcing her close to a beckoning, terrifying edge.

His mouth left her and he surged up her body, his hand still buried between her thighs. She cried out as his mouth closed over her breast once more and he suckled fiercely in wicked concert with the rhythm between her legs.

She broke, simply broke apart, her world consumed in fire as she fell, sobbing, from the precipice, felt his arms close about her and hold her safe, heard his voice soothing her as the firestorm ebbed.

Ash drew back, looked down at Maddy, his bride, his innocent bride, spread before him in delectably wanton abandon, her body still trembling in the aftermath of pleasure, her legs hanging limply over the edge of the bed. He caressed the slick, sensitive flesh and she gasped, shuddering, so sweetly responsive. And his. All his.

'Ash?'

'Yes, love?' Lord, when had he ever said *that* to a woman? Called her that?

Her eyes opened, dazed and vulnerable. 'Was that what you meant by improperly?'

Despite the savage need ripping at his guts, a chuckle shook him. 'Oh, we're getting there.'

He set his hands to the tantalising swell of her hips and murmured, 'Roll over for me.' She didn't resist, but her body was so limp with pleasure that he ended up doing it for her. His hands tightened, curving over firm, smooth globes.

'Ash…?'

The nervousness in her voice, the uncertainty, had him hardening even more with the need to take her. Make sure she knew she was his. Always. And that there was nothing at all 'convenient' about it.

'Yes?' Very gently he opened her thighs, stepped between them and pressed against the pale curves of her bottom, caressing her hips, the suppleness of her waist.

'What…what are you doing?'

Leaving one hand on her hip to steady her, he reached

between her thighs from behind, found the soft, wet heat and stroked, holding her still, leaning over her until his mouth was close to her ear. He licked, nipped gently, and felt her body shudder, heard the little moan as he teased the damp, sweet secrets.

'I'm going to tup you, Maddy.' He wrapped one hand around his erection, guiding it to where she was so tight and hot, and rocked, barely penetrating her. She was all eager, wet, quivering silk. Ready for him, but he wanted her more than ready. He wanted her frantic, desperate, begging for him.

Maddy's lungs seized as he pressed in, no more than an inch, and rocked there. *I'm going to tup you...* Understanding sent a bolt of need flashing through her. She wanted more, needed more, but he held back.

'Ash! *Please.*'

He leaned forward, covering her, until his mouth was by her ear again, his breath hot. Her body trembled, bucking against his weight. 'What do you want, Maddy, love? Tell me.' And he pressed a little deeper so that she cried out, aching for more.

'Touch me!'

'Where, little one? Here?' He nipped at her throat, at the scrambling pulse beneath her ear.

'Inside me,' she got out, her voice breaking.

His strength held her effortlessly, one hand playing

at her breast, the other arm hooked under her belly, his fingers teasing the sensitive nub just above where his shaft promised heaven.

'How do you want me inside you, Maddy?' he whispered. His fingers slid closer to the empty ache he was teasing. 'Like this again?'

'Your—' Her voice broke as he rocked, stroked the taut nubbin so that fire leaped in every vein, need coiling in her belly. 'Whatever you call your pizzle,' she finished.

The word, when he told her, made her shiver. It sounded so hard, uncompromising.

'Say it, Maddy,' he murmured. 'Say it.'

And she did.

'I want you—*all* of you,' she whispered then. 'Inside me.'

'I'm all yours, sweetheart,' he whispered. 'Only yours. Always.'

He gave himself to her, one inexorable inch at a time. Slowly. His voice shook, whether reminding himself or reassuring her, she didn't know. Her body burned as he took all of her, body, heart and soul, with exquisite care until at last he impaled her fully and she sobbed in pleasure.

'You like this?' he asked, moving gently.

She couldn't speak, only moan at the shift of his body inside her, above her, surrounding her.

'And this?' he murmured, changing the angle so that she gasped. 'Or this?'

And her body exploded on a shocked cry as he found that secret place within where delight bordered on pain.

His growl of satisfaction told her he knew. And then there was nothing else, nothing beyond his body taking hers, the wet slide of him inside her and the wicked counterpoint of his fingers. Nothing but the flames building, building inside her until she hung, blind with need, on the edge of that fiery abyss. He held her there, sobbing, shaking, every stroke of his body into hers both a searing delight and an agony of delay.

He pulled back, waited, and she cried out in protest as her body wept for release. He surged back into her and she screamed as she fell, broke and shattered around him.

Ash felt his control snap at her utter surrender. Again and again he took her, without compromise, without restraint, driving deep, deeper into the hot, tight sheath convulsing about him. Consummation, white-hot and relentless, crashed over and through him. He drove in one last time, shuddering with release as he poured himself deep inside her. He hung over her for a moment, dazed, blind with pleasure, and then collapsed onto her soft, trembling body with a groan. Nothing had ever been so good. He was surprised it hadn't killed him.

Drawing on the last of his strength, somehow he got them both onto the bed properly and under the bedclothes. Maddy murmured in sleepy contentment as he settled her into his arms, precisely where she belonged. With a sigh she nestled closer, and one small hand slid over his heart. Steel bands clamped around his chest.

He had no idea if there was a bedchamber prepared elsewhere for him and he didn't care. He was exactly where he wanted to be. Gently he covered the hand over his heart with his own and held it there, holding off sleep. It beckoned, but the delight of having her utterly sated in his arms, completely and irrevocably his, was shockingly precious.

A little while later he felt her stir in his arms.

'Ash?'

'Maddy, love?'

She snuggled closer and his arms tightened as he looked down at her. Firelight gilded her face, even in the shadows of the bed, and his heart quaked as she smiled sleepily up at him. There was nothing even remotely convenient about what he felt.

'That was definitely improperly, wasn't it?'

He brushed his lips against her temple, breathed the

fragrance of warm, soft, utterly pleasured woman. *His* woman. 'Definitely.'

She sighed. 'Apparently I like improper.'

He snorted out a laugh. 'Just as well, under the circumstances. Go to sleep. We can be improper again later.'

Chapter Seven

Christmas Day was a blur of light and laughter to Ash. He took Maddy to church in the morning, along with most of the household. The church was full and bells pealed wildly afterwards as they walked out into the biting wind, surrounded by the warmth of good wishes and blessings.

Mr and Mrs Parmenter insisted on offering brandy at the vicarage. Ash wanted nothing more than to get Maddy back to Haydon. Back home. *Their* home. But she accepted, saying, 'It will give Bets and the rest a chance to get home and put dinner together.'

So he acquiesced and, when Parmenter took him aside, put away his anger at the man's hesitance over marrying them yesterday. This was not a day for anger or grievances.

Parmenter said quietly, 'I was wrong yesterday, Lord Ashton. Very wrong. My good wife took me severely to task. When I thought it through afterwards, your trust in Madeleine shamed me. Our Lord warned us against throwing the first stone. May I ask your forgiveness?'

Ash let out a breath. 'Yes. A confession, sir. I was unsure, too. Oh, not of her,' he went on, seeing Parmenter's surprise. 'But I did wonder if Montfort—' He broke off, clenching his fists.

'Quite,' said Parmenter, his face grim. 'A word for your ear. Be on your guard. My wife is not above listening to the chatter of our housemaids.' He cleared his throat. 'In short, they are all worried that Montfort may still do something foolish.' His hand gripped Ash's sleeve. 'It pains me to gossip, but—'

Ash nodded. 'Thank you, sir. I'll guard her.'

Parmenter frowned. 'Guard yourself, too. You made a fool of him yesterday.' He hesitated. 'I have known Montfort all his life. I dislike speaking ill of one of my flock, but he is not an honourable man.' He flushed. 'Another stone, but there I'll take my chances.'

Maddy had been sure something was bothering Ash as they drove home from church. But when she'd asked he'd denied it. Now, watching him set up a bowl of raisins for a game of Snapdragons with several of the children at one end of the great refectory table after Christmas dinner, she wondered if she had imagined that odd abstraction.

She had not expected marriage to be like this at all. There was nothing convenient about this ache in her heart. Foolishness. How could she have fallen in love with a man she hadn't seen for years? And yet what else could it be that had her bones to melted honey every time he called her love? A word only. Probably a casual endearment he had used with women before.

And yet she could not forget how he had woken her in the night and made love to her again, so gently, so completely, and murmured that sweet word to her as she broke and shattered.

Seeming to realise she was watching, Ash glanced up from pouring warmed brandy over the raisins and met her gaze with a smile that turned her heart inside out before he gave his attention back to the game and the children.

A delighted cry went up as Ash lit the bowl. Maddy let out a breath. He had told her once that men desired women all the time. That it was convenient if they desired each other. So she had to assume that, for him, that was all it was. Desire. Convenience. And it was not his fault if now she wanted more.

The hall rang with laughter and shrieks as, along with Ash, the children snatched raisins from the dish of flaming brandy until the flames subsided and they each had a pile of raisins in front of them. Maddy's mind ranged ahead. Christmas was a time for promises, for hope and joy. Once, long ago, a child had been born who was all that—promise, hope and joy. By next Christmas would they have their own child? Might she already be carrying Ash's child?

'Right. Let's see,' said Ash, counting his raisins.

The children counted theirs, as well. Only one pile looked as big as Ash's.

'I've got twenty,' announced Ash, sitting back in his chair, candlelight gleaming on his hair, and his eyes glinting a challenge at the boy with the biggest pile, who was scowling in concentration.

A moment later there was a triumphant shriek. 'Twenty-one! I've got twenty-one. I beat you, sir!'

Ash narrowed his eyes, examining the challenger's pile. 'Young whelp. You have, too. Well done!' He grinned at the boy, reaching out to ruffle his hair, and Maddy swallowed, imagining him with his own sons. 'You'd better eat them now,' he said, rising. 'You can share mine out.'

He strolled over to where Maddy was sitting by the fire. 'A penny for your thoughts,' he said, bending over her. At her feet, Ketch wagged his tail.

If she said what she was thinking, would it spoil what she already had? Her heart quailed. Falling in love with Ash was going to break her heart. He had married her for convenience and to protect her. It was clear enough that he desired her. Could that be enough for her?

She managed to smile up at him. 'Only a penny? I was thinking that it must be time to retire.' She let her eyelashes drop as his eyes darkened. 'I'm sure we'll be excused.' Her fingers toyed with the lace kerchief about her neck, unknotting it slowly while she held his heated gaze, and then gently drawing it off. 'And I believe I have a favour to return.'

When at last Ash tumbled his wife beneath him on their bed he was hard and aching. God help him if she learned anything more about inciting a man to madness. She'd returned every favour and invented a few more. Now it was her turn.

'I'm going to have you now, wife,' he whispered.

Her smile was Eve incarnate as she yielded sweetly, her arms coming about him as he settled between her thighs.

'I thought it was mutual,' she murmured, and kissed him.

'Maddy,' he whispered, and took her mouth as completely as he took her body.

* * *

Ash woke with a start, unsure what had disturbed him. He'd been dreaming, he thought, but not the usual nightmares. Just an ordinary dream.

The sound came again. A scratching and snuffling at the door. He sat up carefully, trying not to disturb Maddy, snuggled next to him. There was a very faint glow from the fire—enough to see by.

'I think it's Ketch,' she said sleepily. 'Someone must have forgotten to take him to the stables. Just open the door. He'll sleep by the fire if you tell him.'

Ash looked down at her. 'Where does he usually sleep?' he asked suspiciously.

She looked a little self-conscious. 'Well, in here. By the fire, mostly. But sometimes he sneaks onto the bed, and I thought last night—'

He was fairly sure she was blushing. Just as well she had put the dog out last night…. Clearing his throat, he got out of bed and went to the door. Sure enough, when he opened it, there was Ketch.

Ash pointed to the hearth. 'There,' he said, employing his best commanding officer voice.

The dog gave him a very surprised look, but wagged his tail and made for the fire, curling up in front of it and looking hopeful, just the tip of his tail moving.

'Very well,' said Ash, fighting a grin. 'But just remember—the bed is mine.'

The next time he woke up it was to the sensation of something wet and cold nuzzling at him. He cursed as something scratched at him.

'Damn it, dog!'

He opened his eyes to the glow of firelight. Ketch was reared up, one paw on the bed, the other raised, apparently about to nudge him again. Ash sat up, about to explain to the dog exactly where he was making his mistake.

Ketch got down, backed up a little and growled. Then he ran to the door, still growling, and looked back at Ash.

'Does Ketch want to go out?'

Maddy sounded half-asleep.

Was that all it was? A dog needing to go outside? Ash got out of bed, reached for his breeches and shirt and hauled them on.

Maddy sat up, clutching the blankets to her. 'Why is he growling?'

'He doesn't usually growl to go out?'

'Of course not. He stands on me and licks my face!' She threw back the bedclothes.

But the dog had come to *him*. Growling. Something was wrong.

Maddy had flung on her nightgown and was belting her robe about her, sliding her feet into slippers.

'You stay here,' he snapped, with Parmenter's warning in mind. He couldn't believe Montfort would be so stupid, but…

She glared at him, pushing hair out of her eyes. 'This time *you* can save *your* breath. I'm coming with you.'

His mind raced. 'All right. But stay back with Ketch until we know what's going on.' Seeing mutiny in her eyes, he added, 'That's called strategy. Keeping something in reserve in case your first plan doesn't work.'

Her eyes narrowed, but at least she nodded. Strategy, hell. If it was Montfort, he didn't want her anywhere near him.

The door that led from the corridor into the hall was closed. Ash set his hand lightly to the handle, listened. Muffled footsteps sounded. Ash tensed. It sounded as if someone wearing heeled boots was trying not to make too much noise. Only old Bets and Cally Whitfield slept in the house. They didn't wear boots.

He glanced over his shoulder. Maddy stood halfway along the corridor, Ketch's collar gripped in one hand, a candlestick in the other. He held up one hand in a 'no farther' gesture and eased the door open a couple of inches.

The hall was lit only by the fire. The fire they had left banked. Someone had stirred it up again. In the flickering light a man moved around quietly, pouring liquid from a can. He wore a heavy coat and a hat pulled down low over his face, but for a moment the firelight caught his features. *Montfort.*

Ash sniffed. Lamp oil. His gut twisted. The bastard thought he was going to burn them out. Even as he watched, Montfort started laying the trail of oil towards the fire. Ash cursed mentally. He had to try to stop Montfort before he got any closer to the fire. If the blighter was armed, he was in trouble, but there was no time to find his own pistol and load it. By the time he did the hall would be ablaze.

He opened the door fully and strolled in. 'Good evening, Montfort. You're a little late for the Christmas goose.'

Montfort swore and dropped the can. Oil flooded from it but, thanks to the uneven old floor, did not flow towards the fire.

'You're a bloody nuisance, Ravensfell,' he said.

Ash shrugged. 'I do try. The magistrates are going to take a rather dim view of this, you know.'

Montfort laughed. 'The magistrates? They aren't going to hear anything except what a tragedy it was that Lord and Lady Ashton Ravensfell died when Haydon burned to the ground. I'll be chief mourner for my poor little cousin. Might even persuade the courts to award the estate to me.'

He took a pistol from his pocket and trained it on Ash.

Time slowed to a crawl. He was too far into the hall to reach the door. But it didn't matter if he died. He couldn't risk Montfort getting to Maddy, and he had to warn her that the bastard was armed.

'You don't think they'll find it odd that I died in a fire with a pistol ball in me?'

Montfort snorted. 'That's assuming there's enough of you left for them to find.'

Ash gathered himself to rush Montfort. At the very least he'd be a moving target in very poor light....

Terror coursed through Maddy. *Ash. Oh, God. Ash!* She pressed against the wall beside the door, cold all over as she listened, hanging on to Ketch. Low growls sounded in the dog's throat and his hackles were up.

One shot. Unless he had a second pistol, Edward had only one shot, and she'd be damned if she'd let him murder Ash. A distraction—she needed to distract him...

Please, God...

She stepped out into the hall. 'Edward!'

Both men whipped around.

'Maddy! Get *back*!'

Ash's voice rang out, but the pistol was no longer aimed at him, and Maddy released her death grip on Ketch's collar. *'Take!'*

Ketch hurtled low across the hall in a blur of movement and sprang in silent fury. The pistol roared as Edward went down under the dog's weight, the ball

smashing into the doorway beside Maddy. Splinters
flew, stinging her cheek.

Ignoring that, she ran forward, grabbed the crossed
swords down from the wall beside the fire, shaking them
free of the holly. 'Ash! Here!' She flung one sword, hilt
first, and he snatched it from mid-air.

Ash breathed again. He wasn't sure he'd ever stop
shaking after seeing Montfort's pistol trained on Maddy,
but at least he was armed now. He advanced to where
Montfort was curled in a ball, arms over his head, protecting his throat from the dog.

'Call the brute off! Call him off!'

'Lie still, Edward, and I'll call him off,' snapped
Maddy, coming up, sword at the ready. 'But I warn
you—if you try anything else I'll set him on you again.'

'Please! Ow!' Ketch had found an opening and bit-
ten an ear.

'Ketch! Enough. Sit and guard.'

Clearly reluctant, the dog released his quarry and sat,
still growling.

Montfort started to sit up, but cringed back when he
found Ash's sword at his throat. Ketch lunged, snapping.

'Sit.'

The dog sat again on Maddy's command, still growling.

Ash, keeping the point of his sword against Montfort's
flesh, asked, 'Will he obey me?'

'Who? Ketch?' said Maddy. 'I don't know. Why?'

'Because I want you to fetch the men.' He wanted her away from Montfort. Safe.

'Oh.' Maddy smiled. 'Well, if Edward does try to get up, Ketch will take him down again whether I'm here or not. But I don't know if he'll obey if you try to call him off.'

'That,' said Ash, in savage satisfaction, 'doesn't really matter.'

'What in the world—?'

Maddy looked around to see Bets and Cally standing in the doorway that led out to the old garde tower.

'Why,' said Bets, 'that's 'is lordship! And what's that stink of lamp oil?'

'You bloody little *idiot*!' snarled Ash, his face white in the fire's glow as he slammed the bedchamber door behind them half an hour later and rounded on her. 'Walking in like that when the bastard was armed! What the *hell* were you thinking?'

Maddy glared at him. 'That he was going to shoot you!'

Ketch, who had followed them in, made for the bed and slunk under it.

Ash said a couple of words she'd never heard.

'Instead, he nearly shot *you*!' he went on. 'What do

you—? Damn it!' His voice changed. 'Your cheek—there's blood on it!'

Maddy became aware that her left cheek really did sting. She raised a hand to it, surprised. 'Oh. Splinters, I think. The ball hit the door.'

Ash reached her, caught her chin in one shaking hand and turned it. His mouth was a grim line. 'Yes, splinters.'

Maddy let out a breath. 'Well. Nothing to worry about, then.'

His hand tightened on her. 'It could have been your eye, and it could still fester! I should put you over my knee and spank you. I *told* you to stay back with Ketch.'

She lifted her chin. 'You said we were the reserves.'

'What?'

His eyes bored into her, but she held her ground. 'In case the first plan didn't work.' She fixed him with a glare. 'And it didn't. If you even had a plan. He had only one shot, so I thought we had a chance if I could distract him. Hopefully waste the shot.'

His mouth flattened. 'You were nearly killed! What the hell did *I* matter? Sit down while I get the splinters out.'

She sat and he lit every candle in the room, banishing darkness and fear. They were safe. Edward was locked up in the root cellar, with a single blanket and no light and two men on guard. Given that he had tried to burn the house down, his plea for a candle had been dismissed. He would be taken to a magistrate in the morning.

Ash found a cloth, heated water over the fire and dabbed carefully at her cheek. She sat very still, trying not to wince as he searched for splinters in grim silence.

Ash could barely speak for remembering the sickening swoop of terror as Montfort's pistol had swung towards Maddy. Knowing he couldn't reach Montfort in time, believing she was going to die.

At last he spoke. 'I'm not saying your plan wasn't a good one,' he said, each word feeling as though it had been ripped from him. 'But you still shouldn't have done it.'

If a junior officer had handled himself like that in action, coming up with a spur-of-the-moment diversion and counterattack to save a comrade, he'd be commending the young idiot.

But Maddy wasn't a junior officer. She was his wife, and he'd thought she was about to die. He eased his fingertips over her cheek, searching. All the splinters seemed to be gone.

'Can you feel anything?' he asked.

What *he* could feel, tearing at his heart, was a damn sight worse than splinters. He'd have to get used to it because, no matter how painful, he couldn't imagine not loving her.

She shook her head. 'I think you got them all. And, for what it's worth, you *do* matter. To me.' She met his gaze. 'You can be as cross as you like, but I'd do it again.'

He groaned, drew her into his arms. 'I know you would. And it terrifies me. What the hell would you have done if you hadn't had the dog with you?' He shuddered, glancing at Ketch under the bed. A tail thumped. 'No. Don't tell me. I don't want to know.'

Epilogue

Twelfth Night

Supper was over, the household had retired for the night and Ash stood, his arm about Maddy, watching the fire blazing in the hearth of the hall. The remnant of the Yule log had been removed and quenched. It was set safely aside to light next Christmas. Yet the fire still burned—and deep inside him, where it counted, there was still a light burning.

This Christmas, their first together, might be over, but he knew that the candle lit within him would always be there. Waiting, hopeful, even if he could never quite tell Maddy. They had made a bargain to save her home from Montfort. Despite everything, he was not entirely sure she would wish to alter that bargain, and her heart had not been part of it.

'Ash?'

'Yes, sweetheart?'

'I was thinking that it hasn't all been quite as convenient as we intended,' she said.

He snorted. 'I'll admit I didn't count on Montfort's lunacy.' His gut twisted. 'Or yours, for that matter,' he growled. 'Losing you would have been damnably *in*convenient!'

Fear still choked him every time he remembered Maddy facing Montfort's pistol for him. If he hadn't already known what it was he felt for her, that shattering instant would have done the trick.

'*Is* love inconvenient, Ash?'

Everything stilled inside him except the hopeful candle that leaped and shouted in joy. 'I don't think so,' he said at last, choosing his words carefully. 'I've been finding it rather painful, not sure if it's unrequited or not. But no, on the whole it's not inconvenient.'

She turned in his arms, witch-green eyes staring up at him in shock. '*You're* finding it painful?' she demanded. 'But I'm—'

To his absolute horror, the bright eyes filled with tears. 'Oh, Lord! Don't cry, Maddy.'

'I'm not crying.' She sniffed. 'I was telling you that I love you, and—'

'I thought you were telling me love was inconvenient?' he said.

'It is,' she muttered. 'But every time you make love to me I keep nearly telling you, so—' She broke off as he grabbed her wrist and towed her unceremoniously across the hall. 'Where are we going?'

'Bed,' he told her. 'I believe you have something to tell me?'

The smile on her face nearly undid him. 'Oh, I do,' she assured him. 'Am I going to have lots of opportunities to say it?'

'Plenty,' he assured her.

* * * * *